Walking Through
the Dark

Walking Through the Dark

Phyllis Reynolds Naylor

Atheneum

New York 1976

LIBRARY OF CONGRESS CATALOGING IN PUBLICATION DATA
Naylor, Phyllis Reynolds. Walking through the dark.
SUMMARY: The Depression causes Ruth's dream of
college and a teaching career to be no longer certain,
but at the same time it enables her to grow as a person
as she encounters others in difficult situations.
[1. Depressions—1929—Fiction]   I. Title.
PZ7.N24Qa   [Fic]   75-23039
ISBN 0-689-30509-5

Published simultaneously in Canada by
McClelland & Stewart, Ltd.
Manufactured in the United States of America by
The Book Press, Brattleboro, Vermont
Designed by Nora Sheehan
First Edition

To my parents

To my parents

Walking Through
the Dark

CHAPTER 1

November 13, 1931

Dear Diary:

Today Father bought two boxes of apples from someone he knew on the corner of State and Madison. Mother says we'll have to use them for sauce, and I don't even like apples. Some birthday present!

For the first time I can remember, I'm not getting a new dress. Mother made over a dotted swiss of Aunt Marie's, but I don't think it looks right for winter. Oh, well. Maybe it's all because my birthday fell on Friday the thirteenth this time. . . .

3

Ruth gently draped the piece of burlap over her head like a shawl and studied her reflection in the window. Her parents' voices drifted out from the kitchen over the clutter of boxes on the back porch: ". . . a man like him . . . he must have owned stock . . . three girls, and a boy in college . . . what on earth will they do?"

She turned her head slightly and viewed her face from a different angle. A dark brown curl stuck out one side of the burlap, clinging against her cheek. Her eyes, widespread, were smoky there in the half-light of the enclosed porch, and she decided they had a look of tragedy about them.

"Apples?" she whispered to her reflection in the glass. "Would you buy an apple, Mister? Five cents apiece. . . ."

"Ruth," her mother called. "You're letting in cold air. Fill the pan and bring it inside."

Ruth placed a dozen apples in the pan, covered the box again with burlap, and entered the warmth of the kitchen. Her father had finished supper and sat over his coffee, head resting in one hand. For the first time Ruth noticed the faint brown age spots on his scalp, where the hairline receded. They matched the spots on his hands.

"You don't know how lucky we are, little girl," he said to her. "I got those apples from Lewis Solomon."

Ruth washed the fruit in the sink without answering.

"You know how much he was worth a year ago? Fifty thousand dollars. *Fifty thousand.* Today— nothing. Worse than that. In debt. Owes every- body."

"He must have had stock," Mother said again.

It was tiresome. Ruth didn't even know Lewis Solomon. She went into the living room and turned on the Philco. Rudy Vallee was singing "Life is Just a Bowl of Cherries." She sat down on the sofa, stretched out her legs, and contemplated the fact that she was now fourteen and had a million things she wanted to do with her life.

What she wanted to do in general was not waste it. She wanted to feel that each year had gone the way it should, according to what she felt an ideal life should be. What she wanted specifically was college and a teaching career. Right now she felt like an architect drawing up a blueprint for the thir- ties. Nothing was more enjoyable than planning the details of the next seven years—the clubs she would join, the subjects she would take, the grades she would get, the boys she would date, her dormitory room when she went away to college. . . .

"Sometimes, Ruth," Mother once said, "you just have to let life happen. You'll only be disappointed if you try to control it too much."

Wrong, Ruth thought. That was the whole se- cret: making things happen instead of accepting whatever came along.

Perhaps it was the death of her grandmother

the year before that made Ruth think so much about life. Grandmother Wheeler had never gone past fourth grade. She was lively and humorous with an alert mind, but she never left the farm, never went to a library, never—to Ruth's knowledge—read anything but the Bible.

"Make something of yourself, Ruth," her grandmother would say, and that was why each year of school was like a mark on a measuring stick. Each added possibilities that Grandmother Wheeler had never known.

On Saturday, Kitty was waiting at the traffic light, and the girls walked four blocks to the theater. The wind whipped at the dotted swiss beneath Ruth's coat, but she concentrated on the sheen of her legs in the silk stockings Mother had given her, taking extra-long steps so she could admire each foot as it came forward in its black patent pump.

"Everything new?" Kitty asked, looking her over.

"Only the dress and stockings." Ruth held open her coat to show the dress—long waisted with a cloth belt and white buckle. "Was Aunt Marie's." She made a face and wrapped the coat around her again.

"I used to get my sisters' clothes, but I'm taller than they are now," Kitty said. She reached in her pocket and pulled out a little box. "I brought you a present. Happy belated birthday."

6

"Oh, Kitty!" Ruth put an arm around her friend, and they walked on together, moving in step. "When shall I open it?"

"After we get inside."

They rounded the last corner and quickly got in line. Above them, on the marquee, black letters spelled out: "*Cimarron*—Irene Dunne, Richard Dix." Near the door was a poster showing the actress in a long taffeta dress and bonnet, and the leading man in a ten-gallon hat, boots, and holster.

"Oh, Lord, but he's handsome," Kitty breathed. "If I had a man like that, with wavy hair, I'd just sit and run my hands through it."

Inside the theater, the girls sank down in the plush maroon cushions, and Kitty produced a sack of opera cremes, which she'd brought from her father's grocery. That was another advantage of going to the pictures with Kitty.

"Open the present," she said, and watched while Ruth untied the yellow ribbon. "I could have bought you something, but I thought you'd like this even more."

Ruth lifted the lid of the small box. There lay a bracelet of intricately overlapping gold leaves, each leaf tipped with a small green stone.

"Kitty!"

The tall girl scanned her face uncertainly. "Do you like it—really?"

"Oh, I *love* it! But . . . it's so expensive looking."

Kitty beamed, relieved. "It used to be my grand-

7

mother's. She always said to save it for a special occasion, but my arms are so skinny it rides way up to my elbow. Besides, I wanted you to have it."

"Oh, Kitty, you're the best friend I ever had. Honestly."

"That's why I gave it to you."

Ruth slipped the bracelet over her wrist and turned it around and around, watching the small green jewels capture the light of the lamps along the gilded walls. Kitty passed her the bag of chocolate cremes, and Ruth savored the rush of sweetness in her mouth, the softness of the velvet cushions, the company of Kitty. It was a glorious afternoon.

Sitting side by side, Kitty was three inches taller than Ruth. But it was her legs that made her really tower above other girls. Where Ruth's knees reached only halfway between her seat and the one in front, Kitty's knobby kneecaps almost touched the forward row, and her long arms lay tangled awkwardly in her lap like the legs of a young stork. Ruth had bobbed brown hair, but Kitty's was black, and she wore it long and straight at the back with the sides braided over the top of her head, making her seem taller still. She had a long delicate nose, and her eyes and lips were fragile and fine. She reminded Ruth of some of the women in paintings at the Art Institute.

The ceiling lights began to go out a row at a time, and late arrivals scurried for seats. A burst of music

8

came from the speakers as the sound was adjusted. Finally a large square of light appeared on the screen, the curtains opened, and Ruth was lost in the story of another place and time.

"I don't see what was so wrong with it. It's a great picture. It won the Academy Award."

Ruth stood over the hot air register in the living room, her white dress billowing as the heat warmed her legs.

Her father's forehead wrinkled with impatience, and tiny blue veins stood out at the temples. Joe Wheeler was a small man, wiry and nervous, and now he sat on the edge of the sofa as though any moment he would spring forward.

"What's wrong is that you already saw it once! A waste of money!"

"But if I go every Saturday anyway, what difference does it make if I see the same movie twice?"

"I see her point, Joe," Mother commented from the dining room where she was addressing Christmas cards.

"She *has* no point!" Mr . Wheeler transferred his glare to his wife. "Millions of people without the price of bread, and this girl pays to see a movie twice. Like we're so rich we don't miss it. This is a depression, Ruthie! You're fourteen now. Time you understood things like that." He stood up and thrust his hands in his pockets, shoulders hunched.

Ruth squatted down on the register to get her legs closer to the heat, hugging herself. "But if I go every Saturday anyway. . . ." she began.

"*Don't* go every Saturday!" her father exploded. "If you've seen a movie once, save your quarter for something else." He whirled suddenly toward the corner where Ruth's younger sister was sprawled on the rug listening to the radio. "Turn that thing down! Can't even hear *myself* above that noise."

Dawn stared back at him.

"Turn it down, Dawn," Mother urged, giving her a special look.

Joe Wheeler faced his wife. "It's up to you now, Grace. You've got to check how the girls handle their money. Don't spend a dime you don't have to." He bent over and picked up the pages of the *Chicago Tribune*, which had dropped from his lap, folding the edges meticulously together. "We don't know the meaning of want. Lewis Solomon didn't either, and now he's standing out there in his two-hundred dollar suits selling apples. A man never thinks he'll come to that. . . ."

He moved over to the window and stared at the street awhile. Then he went outside to check the car's radiator.

Ruth waited till the door closed behind him. She could hear the scratch of her mother's pen in the next room, and waited till it stopped.

"What's the matter with him, Mother? He's got the worst temper lately."

"He sure does!" Dawn agreed. She turned off the Philco and came over to share the heat with Ruth. "Yesterday he scolded me just because I lost three pennies."

"Your father has a lot to think about right now with business way down," Mother answered. "And he's right. We should be more careful with money. See what I've done? I went over all the Christmas cards we received last year and found eleven that we could use again just by cutting signatures off at the bottom. That's one way we can save—little things like that. It all adds up."

Ruth rested her chin on her knees, unimpressed. "That's what poor people do, Mother." Still, it was doing *something*. Her legs were beginning to tingle and itch from the heat. Dawn was leaning back against the wall. All Ruth could see of her were the baggy tan-colored stockings with wrinkles at the knees.

Dawn caught sight of the bracelet.

"Ruth! Where did you get this?" She knelt down and touched the gold leaves with her chubby fingers, brushing back the wisps of blond hair that fell in front of her eyes.

"Isn't it beautiful?" Ruth held out her arm. "Kitty gave it to me this afternoon as a birthday present."

Mrs. Wheeler got up and came over to look. "Why, Ruth! Her family can't afford presents like that! It looks terribly expensive."

"It is. It was her grandmother's."

"It's beautiful, dear, but I don't think you should have accepted it."

"Why *not?*" Ruth demanded. And suddenly, she'd had enough. There was something so joyless about her parents these days. Without waiting for an answer, she went upstairs to her room, leaving the register to Dawn.

Had her parents always been so somber, she wondered, and she was just noticing it more as she got older? Or was there something about the year, the times, that made them so humorless?

The problem, as Ruth saw it, was that her parents weren't doing what they'd always said they wanted. Father had told her once that he had planned to be a history professor, but hard times and family problems forced him out of college, and he never had the chance to go back. Hard times. It was the excuse for everything.

Mother had always wanted to grow flowers, to own a floral shop, even. And here she was in a house with a small sunless piece of yard in back that wouldn't even produce grass—just a bare dark plot of ground with a tree in the middle where Dawn set up house in the summer. Mother's dream got no further than a row of African violets on the window sill.

Well, Ruth wouldn't let that happen to her. She was going to be a teacher—witty, lively, and enthusiastic—the kind that students crowded around when the lesson was over, that parents called to ask advice, that everyone cried over when she retired. Ruth had never had such a teacher. Only one or two had even come close. And that's why she wanted to be it. There would never be any weak excuses if she didn't.

On Sundays, Kitty Lorenzo went twice to Mass —she and her mother and sisters, all with their long black hair braided neatly in coils on top their heads. It was the one day Ruth seldom saw her friend.

Ruth finished dusting the living room and took the cloth upstairs. Mother liked to have the house clean before they took their Sunday drive so she could look forward to coming back. The nicest part about going anywhere, Mrs. Wheeler believed, was coming home again. Perhaps, Ruth thought, that was why Mother's dreams never came true. She was really afraid to venture out, to try new things.

Dawn trailed after Ruth with the dust mop, and as Ruth did the dresser tops and mirrors, Dawn poked into the corners and under beds and took quick swipes at the closet floors. It was Charles's room they minded, first because the heat was always off, second because he had died in it, and third because Mother kept it just the way it had been when he was alive seven years ago, down to the little slippers beside the bed. He would have been ten now, and Dawn had never known him.

"I think I look like Charles," she said, stopping and staring at his photograph on the dresser.

Ruth glanced at it, running her cloth over the frame. "Sort of. You both have round faces. But your mouths are different."

"What was the matter with him?"

"Pneumonia."

"Do you remember it—when he died?"

"I remember Mother telling me. I remember her crying."

They finished quickly and closed the door behind them. Dawn ran up and down the hall a few times, pushing the mop ahead of her, and the housework, a day overdue, was done.

"Let's go for a ride," came Father's voice from the hallway below, but today it had a ring of duty about it, not of pleasure.

Ruth and Dawn got in the back seat and took turns holding the door shut. The car had been dented two months ago and still had not been fixed. It was easier holding the door than reminding Father to have it repaired.

The raccoon collar on Mother's coat blocked the view out the front, so Ruth watched through the side window. Usually the Sunday route was the same—straight east to the lake, then up through

Jackson Park, Grant Park—past the Field Museum and Buckingham Fountain—still north till they reached Navy Pier. Then they would turn west, into the heart of the city, and finally head south on Halsted, which ran the length of Chicago. But today the Pontiac turned west.

"Joe?" Mother said questioningly.

"We're going to see a Hooverville," Father replied. "It's time they knew what it's like."

Ruth was curious. She'd heard the word at school. No matter what happened, it was blamed on the President. Newspapers used for covers were called Hoover blankets. Shanty towns were Hoovervilles. Father said that if the Mississippi flooded, they'd blame that on Hoover, too. But this time he used the word himself.

"What's a Hooverville?" Dawn asked.

"A place where people live when they don't have homes," her father replied.

"Joe, she's so young . . ." Mother murmured.

"These are hard times, Duchess, and the girls have got to know."

They all fell silent then. When Father called her Duchess, Mother never answered.

It was not as though Ruth had never seen poverty. She had seen the bread lines on Maxwell Street, the soup kitchens, the men asleep under the Michigan Avenue bridge. But somehow it had all seemed transitory. Somewhere, she had felt, there was a

15

home waiting—and after a week or two looking for work, the men would go back to wherever they came from, and get jobs somewhere else.

The houses became grayer and shabbier as the car rattled on, then disappeared abruptly as warehouses and factories took their place. For half an hour Ruth watched as sidewalks gave way to crumbling curbstones, and newstands to broken glass. And suddenly there it was, on a once-vacant lot—a Hooverville built around one side of an abandoned icehouse.

At first Ruth thought it was a city dumping ground. And then she saw people moving about and realized that to them it was home. It was as though the icehouse, beset by old age, had developed tumors that crept out from one wall and oozed people. Sheets of corrugated tin leaned against its walls forming metal tents for the families huddled underneath. A family "hooked on" to its neighbors with whatever it could find—a slab of plywood, a few two-by-fours covered with layers of cardboard, a surplus army tent, a box. . . .

Off to one side, a family lived in a deserted streetcar, the elite of Hooverville.

"Is this it?" Dawn whispered to Ruth.

She nodded.

Slowly the Pontiac circled the lot. Dawn sat with her face against the window, frankly staring, while Mother said nothing, lost, it seemed, in her rac-

16

coon collar. Ruth's eyes searched through the makeshift city, amazed at the desperate creativity of those who slept in concrete drainage ducts or discarded bathtubs, looking for the place where, if such a calamity happened to her, she would choose to make a nest. She realized that only the streetcar would do.

The Pontiac came back to the place where it began and started around the lot a second time.

"Oh, Joe!" Mother said quickly.

"Dad! They'll all stare at us!" Ruth protested, pressing back against the seat to escape their faces. But her father was determined.

"Take a good look," he said. "This is hard times. Don't ever forget it."

As the car moved around again, it was not the housing so much or the makeshift clothing that captivated Ruth, but the faces—dull, blank faces that seemed frozen with poverty.

They were passing a family of four living in an open piano crate. The mother nursed the baby, the father lay either sick or asleep. But standing outside, leaning against her home, was a girl slightly younger than Ruth, staring back at her without blinking. And then, as their eyes met, the girl sneered. Not openly—just a curling of the lips, a narrowing of the eyes, a haughtiness of the brows—and Ruth closed her eyes tightly and did not open them again till they were finally heading home.

17

"Was that really necessary?" Mother asked finally.

"Yes," Father answered. "That was really necessary."

Dawn had heard that poor people ate rats. She believed it. Hoovervilles, she decided, separated the lucky from the unlucky, and if they never had to live in a Hooverville, they'd be okay.

Ruth, however, true to her father's advice, did not forget what she saw. All she had to do was close her eyes and she could conjure up the icehouse and its appendages and the girl by the piano crate. Her mind took it further and wove elaborate fantasies in which she, Ruth Lorraine Wheeler, clothed in burlap, would beg for food at the back doors of her neighbors. She, with her brown ringlets and smoky eyes, would plead for pieces of plywood from construction sites. And, with her feet wrapped in newspaper, she would steal pieces of coal off the back of a truck and win the pity of the policeman who would, of course, arrest her. Oh, she would make a most beautiful beggar.

CHAPTER 2

March 12, 1932

Dear Diary:

They still haven't found Lindbergh's baby. I have the feeling he's dead, and the kidnappers never meant to give him back. Everyone is so sad. All the papers carry stories about it.

Kitty and I walked by the high school this afternoon. It's huge, and I just know I'll get lost on my first day. I hope things get better by fall so I can buy some decent clothes. I'd die if I had to start school in Aunt Marie's old dresses.

The man at the back door had on a shirt, a sweater, and two suit coats, one on top the other. His trousers were spattered with mud, and he carried a bundle of clothes tied with a string. His eyes watered, and he tipped his cap slightly when Ruth answered his knock.

"Mornin', miss. I've had a piece of bad luck and was wonderin' if you could give me somethin' to eat. I'd appreciate it, miss. Sure would."

"Tell him yes," Mrs. Wheeler called.

"Appreciate it, miss. Sure do." The man lowered himself down to the top step, his right leg stuck stiffly out in front of him.

Ruth closed the door to the back porch and returned to the kitchen. It wasn't the first time men had begged at the back door, newspapers stuffed under their coats for warmth. Someone once said, half-jokingly, that every time a freight train stopped, the population of Chicago doubled.

"Dawn," Mother said, "get that last piece of pie and put it on a saucer. Is he your father's size at all, Ruth? We have a couple shirts we could give him."

"No. He's a lot bigger."

"We'll just feed him, then." Mother heated up the breakfast coffee and prepared a tray—a corned beef sandwich, a few green beans, bread and butter, pie. . . .

She took the tray out herself. "Why don't you eat it here in the sun?" she suggested. "I'll put some apples and rolls in a bag for you to take along."

"Much obliged," the man said, and his hands shook as he accepted the tray. "Much obliged, ma'am."

Ruth could see the man from where she sat at the breakfast table. The wind had lined his face into deep creases, and his long gray hair hung shaggy about his neck. She couldn't help staring as he hungrily put half the sandwich to his mouth, shoving at it as he ate till it was all in. She wondered if there was a family waiting for him somewhere, hoping he'd come back with a paycheck. He reminded her of the Hooverville.

The man reminded Mother of Annie Scoates.

"It's time I went through Dawn's things again and took Annie some clothes for the twins," she said. "We'll go out next Saturday, girls. I want you both along to help carry the bags, so don't make any plans. Poor soul. Didn't have much to begin with, and the Depression will take what's left, I suppose."

If there was one thing in the world that Ruth dreaded, it was going to see Annie Scoates.

Her mother, Ruth reflected, was what Father called "lace curtain Irish." Her pride was in the home, and so there were napkin rings on the table at dinner, candles on the table on Sunday, and white doilies on the arms of the chairs in the parlor.

The house itself stood gray and lean, as though making room for the others that crowded the block. Only Mrs. Hamilton's, next door, had been painted recently and had a columned porch along the front and sides. Neither was the house Mrs. Wheeler had dreamed of. Still, it was her fortress, the center of her life, and as long as she had it to come back to after a visit to Hooverville or Annie Scoates, she felt protected from whatever it was that Hoover had done to the country.

It was Mrs. Hamilton who told Ruth's mother about the chalk mark. She was a large woman, with a cheerful, but reserved smile, who always wore crepe dresses and a net over her graying hair.

"That man on your back steps this morning," she remarked hesitantly, "did he do any work for you, Grace?"

"No, I didn't ask him to," Mother replied, shoving a clothespin over the edge of the sheet, which flapped on the line.

The lady in crepe pulled her sweater more tightly about her. "It might be unwise, dear, to just feed them for nothing. You know he chalked you."

"Chalked me?"

"Yes. Halfway down your sidewalk he reached over and made a large X. You'll have a real parade of them now, I'm afraid. They stick up for each other. I'd have Dawn go out and erase it."

Dawn rubbed it out with her foot, but every few days another man came, and Mrs. Wheeler always fed them. She could not imagine doing otherwise.

Her mother, Ruth sometimes decided, had not quite caught up with the thirties. She still wore her reddish-brown hair piled high and somewhat frizzled, unlike the short bobs that were popular. Long wisps dangled here and there, giving her the habit of always tucking something in. She was not really good looking, yet she was handsome in her own way. Her face was square and her eyebrows came down low over deepset eyes. But she walked with such composure that she seemed almost haughty, and it was this, plus the little touches she insisted upon about the house, that sometimes prompted Father to refer to her as "The Duchess."

The one person who most appreciated the napkin rings and the formalities was Kitty Lorenzo. Two or three times a month she would stay at the Wheeler home overnight, more often than Ruth stayed at hers. The family enjoyed having Kitty at the table, for she sat in Charles's chair and filled the vacant spot beside Ruth. She was there one Friday night in March.

Mr. Wheeler kept the plates stacked in front of him. He stood at the head of the table in his suit and tie and put small amounts of everything on each plate, passing it on.

"My father says it's a good thing he has all daughters because he couldn't feed sons in a depression," Kitty said.

"Pity for you there isn't one about to pin your

ears back," Father teased, smiling faintly. "How many sisters do you have, Kitty? Two? Three?"

"Four."

"Four! Five daughters in one family? Good Lord. Your father's in the wrong business. Should have bought himself a garment factory."

Kitty laughed.

"How on earth do you manage in one apartment?" Mother asked, nodding firmly to Dawn who was questioning her Brussels sprouts.

"Well, two of my sisters are married. That leaves only Vera and Rose and me. We manage."

"You want to hear a crazy story?" Father sat down and began cutting his meat. "One of the salesmen told it to me. Said he's got a brother-in-law over in Cicero living in a three-bedroom apartment. Well, they've taken in the wife's parents and the husband's parents, and have two kids of their own. Along comes a cousin. Out of work. They tell him there's no room. 'Just let me sleep in the bathtub till I find a job,' he says. Well, they can hardly turn him out. So he takes a sofa pillow and a blanket and makes himself comfortable in the bathtub. Pulls the shower curtain around the tub and he's all set.

"Early next morning one of the grandmas gets up and goes in the bathroom, forgetting that someone's in the tub. Next thing the cousin knows, he hears water running in the sink and somebody brushing her teeth. He doesn't want to say anything to embarrass her, see, yet he's afraid if she opens the curtains and sees a body in the tub, she'll faint. So he lays there figuring what to do.

"Suddenly the old woman starts singing to herself, 'Love's Old Sweet Song,' just as chirpy as you please. So he waits till she gets to the chorus—'Just a song at twilight, when the lights are low . . . ,' and when she gets to, '. . . and the flickering shadows,' he starts humming, harmonizing, you know, 'softly come and go. . . .' By the end of the chorus he's singing full voice—flat on his back in the bathtub. Well, the old woman's voice begins to waver, and the last few words sort of die out. There's a long silence. Then he hears footsteps tiptoeing across the floor and the door opening and closing gently. He never did figure out which old gal it was, and the grandma herself isn't telling."

Mrs. Wheeler threw back her head with laughter, the tangled red hair disappearing as her chin came up. Ruth loved to see her mother laugh like that. Father enjoyed the story so much that he repeated the last line. "Never did figure out which old gal it was, and the grandma herself isn't telling."

"May we never come to that," Mother said. "I wonder if it actually happened."

"Sam says it did. But then, he knows a lot of stories."

"Kitty, did you ever see a Hooverville?" Dawn asked, making a bridge of her knife and fork. "We did, and we saw a whole family living in a bathtub. Honest."

"A whole *family?*"

Mother nodded. "It's strange, you know. This story about a cousin sleeping in the bathtub—we pity him, and yet at least he had a roof over his head. The family in Hooverville had nothing but a piece of cardboard. And I imagine there are a lot of folks who envy that family their bathtub. There are some who don't have anything at all between them and the mud on the ground."

The best part of the evening for Ruth was after Dawn had gone to bed—pudgy Dawn with the pajamas that always rolled up on one leg, who settled herself outside Ruth's room, listening, with her ear to the crack under the door, giggling and waiting, it seemed, to be caught.

But after her small sister was tucked in bed and Mother and Father turned on the radio, Ruth and Kitty had the kitchen to themselves to make popcorn. They would make a huge pan of it to carry upstairs. Then they lay facing each other on the lavender chenille bedspread, the popcorn between them, and dreamed about high school and how it would be.

The girls had met in seventh grade, refugees from spinster sixth-grade teachers who thought nothing of slapping palms and knuckles twice with a ruler for talking aloud in class. To Ruth, arriving from a sixth grade two blocks away, and to Kitty, who was transferring from a Catholic school her parents could no longer afford, junior high would be a haven from all the rules and regulations that had made their lives miserable.

To the horror of both, the rules were even stricter in junior high. The teachers were even older and more set in their ways. They expected silence in the halls, obedience in the classroom, and dress becoming to young ladies and gentlemen. The girls served out their three years as a prison sentence, comforting each other, and yearned for high school to set them free.

"They've got a gym teacher who was a tap dancer once—Miss Faisdel," Kitty said, holding one hand high above her mouth and dropping the popcorn in, a kernel at a time. "Miss Faisdel—doesn't it sound Arabian or something? Rose had her, and said that sometimes after school she dances in the gymnastics room, and if she really likes you, she lets you come in and watch. And she goes out with the history teacher who's absolutely marvelous!"

It sounded like the very teacher Ruth had been looking for all her life. She wished suddenly that her own name was more romantic. Miss Wheeler. Would students ever crowd around a teacher named that?

"I know just what I want to wear on my first

day," Ruth said, turning on her stomach and resting her chin in her hands. "I want a light blue dress with cape sleeves and two rows of small buttons down the front. I saw it in a magazine."

"Rose is going to let me wear her yellow sweater," Kitty said. "But just watch. It will be hot as Texas the first day of school, and then I can't. Rose said that girls used to have to wear baggy bloomers in gym class, but Miss Faisdel let them push the bloomers up, and now the gym dresses all have shorts underneath instead of bloomers."

"You can take walks between classes, too," Ruth added. "You can even eat your lunch outside. And sit on the wall and smoke."

"Are you going to smoke?"

"No. Are you?"

"I don't think so. Rose said it would cave in my chest and make me permanently flat. But Vera smokes, and she's big as anything."

Ruth sat up and leaned against the brass headboard, looking over at Kitty. One thing Kitty had going for her were her dimples—beautiful dimples. No matter how tall and ungainly Kitty grew, Ruth decided, she would get by because of those dimples. Besides, Kitty was the only one of the two who had ever been kissed—*really* kissed. Not just a quick peck on the cheek by somebody in second grade.

"What was it like, Kitty—really?"

"What?"

"When Bill Stedman kissed you."

"Oh—that." Kitty ate another handful of popcorn and thought about it. "Well—wet, for one thing. I mean, his mouth was sort of open. And he pressed his lips real hard against mine and sort of moved his head from side to side—to make sure he got the corners, I guess."

"Did you like it?"

"Yes." Kitty stopped chewing a moment, remembering. "And when he finished, you know what he did?"

"What?"

"He did it all over again." She laughed.

Ruth drew up her knees and wrapped her arms around them. "When I get kissed—really kissed—I want to remember it all my life. I hope it's a romantic place, with the moon and a river and everything."

Kitty frowned. "I guess that's what was wrong with Bill Stedman. He did it in an alley."

"Whatever happened to him?"

Kitty shrugged. "He stopped growing and I didn't."

"Listen, Kitty, we've got to plan it. I mean, people have to work to make things happen."

"What things?"

"We've got to get you introduced to the high school basketball team."

"Good. See what you can do. Tell them you know a tall skinny girl who wants to be mascot."

"Kitty, I mean it. We'll find out if one of them has a sister or something and get her to introduce you around. You've got a beautiful face, Kitty! You really do! Besides, everybody double-dates. That's what the girls say. I want us to go out together all the time. I wouldn't be so scared of what to say."

"What makes you think *I've* got all the answers?"

"Well, you have sisters, and they know."

"Yes, but they don't go along on a date. And it's no good knowing what to say if you don't find out till after the guy goes home."

On Saturday, Joe Wheeler went to work earlier than usual. Ruth woke to find him already gone. Mother was filling shopping bags with shoes and skirts and dresses, and Ruth knew it was the day for Annie Scoates. Carrying their huge bags to the Illinois Central Railroad, they purchased their tickets and waited on the platform for the electric train to come round the bend.

Once inside, they sat together on a side seat, Mrs. Wheeler, Ruth, and Dawn, backs to the window. Ruth kept her bag on the floor, braced on either side with her feet.

"We look like refugees," she complained in a

whisper. "Everybody will think we've been to the 'Sally.'"

Mrs. Wheeler did not even turn her head. She held it high above her coat collar, looking straight ahead. "There are families who would be glad to get clothes from the Salvation Army, Ruth. When I think of the comfort these things will bring to Annie and her children, I don't really mind what people think."

Dawn turned around to look out the window and her bag fell over. An assortment of underpants and socks spilled out into the aisle, and Dawn scrambled to pick them up. Ruth blushed and turned away.

It wasn't that she disliked Annie or didn't want to help her. If she could send their contributions by parcel post, Ruth herself would carry them to the post office. She had never minded Annie when the small freckled woman worked for them—liked her, in fact. Twice a week the scrawny lady had arrived at eight in the morning to do the breakfast dishes, tidy up, and wash or iron or do whatever special chore Mother had set out for her. Annie's gray-blonde hair was always unkempt, and her old dresses had rips under the arms or spots on the front, but somehow it hadn't bothered Ruth because Annie was there in the Wheeler house, always entertaining the girls with her stories.

Annie had been with the Wheelers the day

Charles died. It was she who had held Ruth on her lap when the doctor went in the second floor bedroom with his little black bag, and Ruth remembered how Annie had hugged her tightly and rocked her against the sound of Mother's sobbing.

It was later, when the worries began, that Annie Scoates came only once a week instead of two. They were worries Ruth didn't understand at the time—talk about mortgage money and credit and Grandma Wheeler and the way things were going at the furniture store. Finally Mother told Annie she couldn't afford her at all. She gave her a sack of oranges, fruitcake, coffee, and strawberry jam and walked back to the train with her. From then on, Ruth and her mother did the housework alone, and lately Dawn had been helping.

All this was bearable, however—the scrubbing of the bathtub, sorting the clothes, dusting the china closet. . . . It was the one or two trips a year to Annie's house that Ruth detested, and now, as they sped past Riverdale and Harvey, she wondered why it always seemed so awful.

It was the smell, for one thing. Ruth hadn't remembered Annie Scoates smelling when she had worked for them. But in Annie's two-room house, her nostrils were always assaulted with a peculiar odor that lingered long after she'd left, and it made her sick.

"Why *does* it smell like that?" Ruth asked her mother once.

"When you can't afford a hot water tank, and have to heat your water on the stove, bodies and clothes just don't get cleaned as often as they should," Mother replied.

To Ruth, that was no answer. The fact that Annie and her house smelled was the most awful thing she could imagine. It was not only the odor, however. There were the children—ugly, sickly children who stood over by the wall with their runny noses and dirty undershirts, and stared. Sometimes Ruth went outside and walked around the dirt yard just to get away from it all. Then the sickly twins with their bowed legs would follow and stare some more. Dawn, however, never seemed to mind. She would seek out the old rubber tire that hung from a tree, and sometimes Annie's older boy would push her.

They reached Hazel Crest, and got out. Sometimes an old horse-drawn milk wagon was waiting at the platform as a sort of taxi, but today the milk rounds had not been completed, so Mrs. Wheeler and her daughters had to walk up the road to Annie's, almost a mile away. There were other two-room houses along the road, unpainted and unrepaired. Now and then a face without expression stared frankly out a window, watching them pass.

Dawn began to huff, hoisting her bulging sack to the other arm. She walked pigeon-toed in her scuffed brown shoes, and one garter dangled beneath her skirt, empty of stocking. A dog began barking from the steps of one of the shacks, and Ruth thought what a sight they must be: *some in rags and some in tags and one in a silken gown.*

"What if Annie's not there?" she ventured.

"Then we'll leave the things on her porch, and she'll know who they're from," Mother answered.

Ruth hoped that Annie Scoates would be gone. She prayed that they would find the windows boarded up and a note on the door saying that she and the children had gone back to Tennessee. But as soon as they turned in the yard, the door opened and a cross-eyed girl of three stared out. Instantly she was joined by another, and finally by short, gaunt Annie, herself, in a dirty dress and sweater, one eye half-closed with either infection or blindness.

Silently she waited till they were almost on the porch, as though she couldn't make out who they were. Then her face broke into a wide smile, showing her blackened teeth, and she threw open the door and stretched out one scrawny arm, grinning at Ruth and Dawn:

"Bless you, Miz Wheeler! You all come on in!" She took the bags of clothes and placed them on the bed. "Ruth, girl, let me look at you. Well! A young lady, that's what you are! A right smart young lady! And Dawn! Why, you ain't a baby at all!" She reached around behind her and pulled out Jeanette and Polly. "Here's my twins!" she said proudly. "They're growin' too."

34

"Why, they certainly are!" Mrs. Wheeler sat down in a chair by the table. "The last time I was here, Jeanette had broken her arm."

"Lord, she's near broke a leg, too, since then." Annie took their coats and laid them on her bed also. Ruth hoped she wouldn't offer them anything to eat, and was relieved that she didn't.

At first Ruth thought perhaps the smell was gone. But then Annie closed the door behind them and instantly her nose was filled with the penetrating odor of leftover food, urine, and something else she could not name—a smell almost of sickness.

This time Dawn noticed.

"Hey, what's so stinky?" she asked, surprised at the odor.

Neither Mother nor Annie answered. Mother reached out and clasped Dawn's arm firmly as she went on talking to Annie.

"I put in some things for you too, Annie," Mother said, nodding toward the bags on the bed. "I know you're several sizes smaller, but maybe you can cut them down."

"I sure appreciate 'em, Miz Wheeler. Don't worry. I'll make do."

"How are things going?"

At this, Ruth was surprised to hear Annie Scoates laugh—a sudden, desperate laugh that she seemed to have been holding back half her life. She leaned forward, her elbows on the table. "Well, we're down just about as low as we can get," she said.

"Have to dig a hole to get any lower. Yes, Ma'am. Have to dig a hole." She seemed to have laughed so hard it brought tears to her eyes. But suddenly the laughter stopped and the tears remained. "If it was May," she said at last, wiping one hand across her trembling lips, "I could get my garden growin' again. Nothin' out there right now but dirt."

"Do you have any food in the house at all, Annie?"

"Oh, yes, Ma'am. We got some. A neighbor, he give me some beans, a little cornmeal, and hog fat. We got to sift out the bugs first, though—worms and weevils both. Sometimes the kids won't eat it, it turns their stomachs so, but they get hungry enough, they come get a piece of cornbread. I tell 'em any bugs get through to that oven, the heat will clean 'em up, but who wants to feed their children worms?"

Ruth let out her breath as slowly as she could, then quickly breathed in again. She sat down next to her mother.

Dawn had walked over to a side window and was writing her name in the steam on the glass. The twins followed and began making marks of their own.

"At least it's warm in here," Mother said. "I'm glad of that."

"Plenty of trees back there. Timothy—I send him out to get sticks. He's a strong boy now. Can even use the ax. Don't know what I'd do without him. Goes way out to the railroad yard sometimes and brings me back coal. I know he shouldn't, but they all do, you know. Soon's a train stops, the men climb up and throw coal down to the children to carry home. I won't let him climb up, though. And sometimes the men get mad if he picks up what they threw down for themselves. Got beat up once for it."

A baby cried from the next room and Mother looked quickly at Annie, but the small woman had already jumped up to go get it, avoiding Mother's eyes.

"A *baby*, Annie?"

Annie disappeared in the next room and came out with a small red-faced baby wrapped in a quilt.

"Miz Wheeler, this is my last one," she said, as though it were a pledge, and still her eyes avoided Mother's. "Benjamin. That's his name."

"Oh, Annie," Mother said. "That's the last thing you need." But she stretched out her arms nonetheless and took the baby and held him for a moment before giving him back to be nursed.

Annie Scoates unbuttoned the front of her dress and offered a limp breast to the baby. "My last babe," she said again. "Lord knows I didn't ask for it, but now that he's here I'll do what I can for him."

"These are hard times, Annie," Mother nodded. "It's hard all over. People we've known—wealthy people, some of them—have lost everything. Men jumping out of windows because they've lost their entire fortunes. It's the fear. Everybody's frightened at what might happen next. Nobody knows."

Annie shook her head, smiling faintly. "Ain't nothin' as scared as a million dollars. For me, it's always been Depression. Just a little worse now than before, that's all. Don't bother me the banks closing, 'cause I never had nothin' in 'em. Can't understand a man jumpin', though. He's got a wife and children to come home to, ain't he? Never had nothin' to lose, so it don't affect me the way it do some folk. My house could burn down, but long as my children were safe, all I'd miss was a couple coats and an old iron skillet." She laughed again, bit her lip, and sat looking down at the baby.

The door opened and a boy of eleven stepped into the room. He was surprised and embarrassed to find visitors, and stood numbly, hands dangling.

"Timothy, how are you?" Mrs. Wheeler said at once.

"'Member Miz Wheeler, Timmy?" Annie Scoates said. "Used to work at her house, and once or twice I took you along. You remember that?"

Timothy shook his head.

"Tree fell down back there, Ma," he said. "Goin' to take the ax and chop it before some of the men git it."

"He's a fine big boy I got," Annie said as Timothy scurried back outside and disappeared in the woods. "Looks just like his father, too."

"What about your husband, Annie? Do you get any help from him?"

"Lord, haven't heard from the man for six, seven years. There's been two more of 'em since, and they both of 'em left me. Just like he did. Last summer one come back for a week and brought me a sack of pecans from Georgia. Imagine that! Pecans! Kids didn't know what to do with 'em."

I want to leave, Ruth screamed in her head, averting her eyes from the grease-spattered wall above the stove, the holes in the linoleum on the floor. *I want to get out in the air and never come back here again.* She stood up and moved over to the window.

Dawn had gone outside to find the swing, but it had fallen during the winter. She was amusing herself by propping a board up on the woodpile and running up and down it. The twins followed her example, arms outstretched, feet bare in the cold March air.

"Yes, you have a pretty girl here," Annie Scoates was saying again, looking at Ruth. "She'll have boyfriends enough."

"I imagine so," Mother said.

"Have you started high school, Ruthie?"

"No. Next fall."

"That's the thing to do—get yourself an educa-

39

tion. 'Course, the way things is now, college men are out digging ditches. But when the hard times is over, there'll be a place for young folks that finish school. That's what I tell my Timothy."

Ruth caught her mother's eye and silently mouthed, "Let's go."

"I imagine we'd better get started home so I can get dinner on," Mrs. Wheeler said, standing up. "I'm glad to see you're well, Annie. Hope a lot of Dawn's things are right for the twins. There's a spring coat they could use, I know. No, don't get up. Look, the baby's almost asleep. You take care, now."

"Bless you," said Annie.

Ruth was the first one out the door, and she took a deep breath of air, but even the yard had an odor.

"We're going, Dawn," Mrs. Wheeler called. "Good-bye, Annie. See that those girls get all the milk they need."

Jeanette and Polly ran back inside, and Ruth was glad when the door closed and shut them off from her.

I wouldn't be like Annie! Ruth told herself fiercely. *I wouldn't! I'd clean myself and the children and go from house to house till somebody took me in. I'd beg if I had to, and work and do anything, but I wouldn't smell. I wouldn't smell!*

Joe Wheeler did not get home in time for dinner.

He was not home by seven either. At eight o'clock Mother called the furniture store. Someone said that Father was on his way.

The pork roast was heated again, and the potatoes warmed. Ruth sat at one end of the dining room table working on a chart for geography. Dawn was cutting out paper dolls over the hot air register. She delighted in fastening a long paper bridal dress on the doll and then releasing it over the stream of air from the furnace, watching doll and dress flutter delicately down.

The whole setting on this particular evening was one that Ruth remembered for a long time afterwards because it was so normal, so safe, so happily ordinary—Dawn humming to herself, Mother puttering about the kitchen. . . .

The Pontiac pulled up in front of the house. Father's footsteps sounded on the steps, the porch, and then the front door opened and closed. The hangers in the closet clanked as he hung up his coat.

"Joe?" came Mother's voice from the kitchen. "I finally called the store, and they said you were on the way. Meat's a little dry, I'm afraid."

There was no answer. Mother walked out of the kitchen into the front hall. There was more silence. Ruth remembered that silence well. And then she heard her father's dull, dead voice saying, "The store's been sold, Grace. They've let the salesmen go."

"Sold!" Again the silence. "But all those men with families. . . . Who bought it?"

"Man from Indianapolis. He's bringing in his own men."

"But . . . you? . . ."

"I'm out of a job too, Grace. After nineteen years, I've lost my job."

CHAPTER 3

May 10, 1932

Dear Diary:

Father went to the employment office again today. He said he waited in line for three hours, just to find out that they still don't have anything. I'm glad there's only one more month of school, because my shoes are awful. Clyde Heidelberger was waiting outside of history. Kitty says she can tell that he likes me. She said that he turned around and watched me all the way to the pencil sharpener. Clyde asked where I live. I hope he doesn't come over and find Dad at home. I told him Father was working at Smythes.

No one, in Ruth's opinion, went about things right. Annie Scoates went on having babies when she should have been trying to find work; Mr. Maloney, next door, sat on the steps of his landlady's house for hours at a time, staring vacantly at the street; and now Father lay on the davenport each evening after dinner, saying nothing. He did not sleep. His eyes were always open, fixed on the ceiling. Occasionally he rubbed his chest, as though thinking made it hurt. It was as if everyone had lost the will to try. What was wrong with people that they just accepted whatever came along? Why didn't they fight? Why didn't it make them angry? They acted as though the Depression were their own private problem.

She went over to the bay window in the living room to look at Mr. Maloney again. He had been sitting in that same position, elbows on his knees, when she got home from school that afternoon. Round-faced, plump, with a white mustache that hung down in two long shafts either side of his mouth—hair so white-blond that even his eyelashes had no color. Now dinner was over, and he still hadn't moved. If he were dead, she reasoned, he would have toppled over. Unless rigor mortis had set in. It sickened her. If rigor mortis had set in, they would have to bury him that way, with his elbows on his knees. Perhaps she should go tell Mrs. Hamilton. It was the landlady's responsibility. . . . And suddenly the man moved, turned his head and spit in the grass, and Ruth went back to the dining room, closing him out of her mind.

Father was still on the sofa. He lay so tense it seemed that his head was scarcely touching the cushions. He was talking now, however, and that made Ruth feel better; she wasn't so shut out. She opened her history book and sat down at the table, pretending to read.

"Nineteen years, Grace. Like I was the delivery boy or something. 'Listen,' I said to Ralph Lawson. 'I been manager of this store since your father opened it. You tell this guy from Indianapolis I go with the deal. I know the merchandise. I know what moves. What they're buying in Chicago isn't the same as what they buy in Indianapolis. He'll need someone who knows the neighborhood—all the old customers.' "

Ruth waited, her eyes closed. Was this all he ever had to say? How could Mother stand it? Six times . . . seven . . . a dozen times, almost every day, they had heard the story, and still he had to tell it again, as though a poison swelled up inside of him and came out each time with the telling.

Mrs. Wheeler bent over the darning needle and

45

studied the sweater in her hand, turning it this way and that. She said nothing.

". . . but he says, 'Joe, I tried, but no luck. I wanted him to take the salesmen too, but he said he was bringing in all his own men. I told him he should at least take Wheeler, then—good manager, I told him—but he said all his men were managers.'" Father put his hands under his head and propped it up. "Huh. Every salesman you meet now was a manager once. Who the hell are the managers anymore? The company presidents? Doesn't matter what you were, tomorrow you could be out on the street selling apples. Remember Lewis Solomon. It doesn't add up, Grace. Just doesn't add up."

"I'm sure Ralph Lawson tried his best to get the new owner to keep you," Mother said finally. "I really believe he tried."

"Ha." Mr. Wheeler sat up and swung his legs over the side of the couch. "When a manager for nineteen years gets kicked out in the street, it says something about the company. Says something about the merchandise they sell. Lawson should have included me in the contract. Smythes wouldn't have kicked me out. Smythes has class. And to think I could have had a job there once. Fifteen years ago they tried to get me. But I said why should I give up being manager to be a salesman again? I'll stay. I was a fool. Should have gone with the high-class stuff and worked my way up. I could have, too. . . ."

46

"Dad, why don't you try Smythes now?" Ruth ventured.

"I've tried every damn furniture store in Chicago," Father muttered. He leaned back, tipping his head over the frame of the couch, and sighed. "Some places the salesmen won't even tell you who the manager is. Won't even show you to his office. Afraid somebody else will take their place."

"Ralph did give you a bonus along with your severance pay," Mother murmured. "We can be grateful for that."

"How long do you think we can live on that, Grace? How long?"

It was a question no one wanted to answer, and Mother did not try.

The awful thing about Clyde Heidelberger having her address was that he could show up any time. From the moment Ruth got up in the morning till she went to bed at night, Clyde could be wheeling up the street on his bicycle or approaching the front steps. Whether she were groping down the hall in her pajamas, sitting sleepy-eyed over her toast at breakfast, or scrubbing the bathtub on Saturdays, Clyde could ring the doorbell and ask if she were in.

It was a great inconvenience. It meant rising early on weekends and dressing instantly. It meant having her best kimono handy on her way to and from the bath. It meant checking her face and hair constantly, pulling the wrinkles up out of her stockings, and keeping a fresh coat of Tangee on her lips. Once, when she was cleaning the downstairs closet, she caught a glimpse of herself in the hall mirror. Her hair was tangled softly around her ears and shone auburn at the ends where the sun hit it. There was a touch of color high on her cheeks, and one dark lock of hair broke into spontaneous ringlets at her temple. If only Clyde would come then. If only, at that very moment, the bell would ring and he would find her in this careless state of natural beauty.

"Why on earth didn't you give him your phone number instead?" Kitty asked as they dressed for gym in their curtained cubicle, hiking the poplin bloomers up over the belt to make them shorter. "If he had your number, at least he could call first and tell you he was coming."

"He didn't ask!" Ruth moaned. "It would seem like I was being eager."

"Well, he could always look your number up in the directory, I guess."

"He doesn't know Daddy's first name." Ruth stuffed her sweater and skirt in the locker and banged the door. Suddenly she stood motionless, arms dangling at her sides. "Kitty! What if he calls Smythes?"

"What?"

"What if he calls Smythes to find out Daddy's first name?"

48

"Why would he do that?"

"Because I told him Daddy works there."

Kitty sat back down on the bench exasperated. "So why did you tell him that? You want him to think you get all your furniture there? High-class snoots?"

"Oh, Kitty, I just want him to like me, that's all."

Kitty snorted and started up the basement stairs to the gym, towering over the other girls on her long thin legs, and Ruth hurried to catch up.

"Listen, Kitty, you've got to give him my phone number."

"You're batty, Ruth. All he has to do is check all the Wheelers in the directory until he finds one at your address."

"But what if he doesn't think of that? What if there are too many Wheelers listed and he gives up? What if he just decides to call Smythes instead? Oh, Kitty, please!"

"But how, Ruth?"

"I don't know, but you've got to figure out a way. You don't know what it's like thinking that any minute he could ring the doorbell."

The girls took their places at inspection, their toes primly touching the yellow line, arms at their sides, eyes straight ahead. A tall, speckled woman in a blue sweater and bloomers walked slowly down the row of girls, taking roll.

"You know what my sister says, Ruth?" Kitty whispered.

"What?"

"That the most important thing is to tell a boy the truth. She says if you don't, you'll have a mess of lies to clean up later."

"But maybe Dad *will* get a job at Smythes. I mean, I just don't want him to think we're beggars or anything just because Dad's out of work. Naturally, he wouldn't take just any old job. And we've got a lot of money to hold us over. We're not *poor* or anything. I wouldn't want Clyde to think that."

"Kitty Lorenzo," called out the tall woman with the whistle around her neck.

"Present," chirped Kitty.

"Ruth Heidelberger," Ruth whispered under her breath.

"What?" Kitty whispered back.

"Ruth Heidelberger. Mrs. Clyde Heidelberger. Mr. and Mrs. Clyde D. Heidelberger. How does it sound, Kitty?"

"Pretty fast, if you ask me."

There was a knock on the back door at dinner. Ruth sprang from her chair and was halfway upstairs to change her dress when she heard Mr. Maloney's voice, and sheepishly took her seat again. Mrs. Wheeler brought their neighbor into the dining room.

"We're just having dinner. Can't you eat with us?" she insisted.

"No, Ma'am. Didn't know you were eating. Wouldn't have come over."

"Please let me fix an extra plate."

"Oh no, thank you. I've had my supper. You go right ahead, and I'll just sit for a moment." He took a chair beside the buffet. Mrs. Wheeler poured a cup of coffee and put it in his hand. The family resumed eating.

"How are things, Ed?" Father asked, methodically cutting the small piece of ham on his plate. "Any luck yet?"

"That's what I came to see you about." The moon-faced man with the walrus mustache and white eyelashes was speaking faster and leaning forward. His jaws hung down over his shirt collar and shook as he spoke. His nose was large and more purple than Ruth had remembered it. Thin wisps of hair in the center of his balding head moved this way and that. He did not drink the coffee, but continued to hold it gingerly in one rough hand.

"Was downtown to see about a job haulin' dirt," he said, "and a man came up to me in line and asks am I lookin' for work. Sure, I tells him. He's manager of an office building over on LaSalle, and he takes me over and explains the elevators to me. He's lookin' for another operator, six days a week, nine to three, thirty-five dollars. I can hardly believe it. I'll have me a stool to sit on, too. He asks me all kinds of questions—when my wife died, you know,

51

and where I worked last—and has me fill out a paper. He says I seem like the reliable sort. Can start me on Saturday, he says."

"Now that's good news, Ed," Father said. "We're really glad to hear it. Inside work—steady. Really good news."

"We're so happy for you," Mother said.

"If there's nobody waiting to get on, can you ride it up and down by yourself?" Dawn wanted to know.

Mr. Maloney broke into a grin, displaying a large vacant space where some of his teeth were missing. "Can, I suppose. You come by, and I'll give you a ride for free."

They all laughed. Mr. Maloney stopped smiling abruptly and leaned forward again. He set the untouched coffee on the buffet and cleared his throat.

"Only problem is, I've got to come up with fifty dollars by tomorrow for the uniform. It's a fancy building, it is—all the operators wear green suits with gold braid, you see. 'I don't have fifty dollars,' I tell the manager. But he says I could borrow it maybe, and pay it back with my first two weeks' salary. Now I'm not an askin' man, and I'd live on dirt before I'd go beggin'—you know that, Joe. But I see a good chance here, and was just wonderin' if you folks could possibly lend me half. Mrs. Hamilton says she'll loan me the rest, and I'll pay you back first."

The Wheelers exchanged glances.

"Mind, there's no other way I'd ask for a loan, except I could pay it back in a couple weeks. If you could just see your way clear to lend me twenty-five...."

"Times are hard all over, Ed," Father said. "I'm still waiting for word on a job myself. Why doesn't the manager pay for the uniform and deduct it from your pay?"

"He says they can't do that—sometimes the operator just takes off and sells the uniform somewhere before it's paid for and buys whiskey. Says they used to do it that way, but it didn't work out." Mr. Maloney's face flushed with the intensity of his request. "Give me a couple weeks to get on my feet, and I'll pay you interest on it. Ten percent. Whatever you say. And maybe I can do the same for you sometime."

"Sure, Ed. I know you would." Joe Wheeler reached for his wallet and took out fifteen. "It's all I've got on me. Grace, would you get the rest from the box?"

Silently Mother went upstairs and returned with ten. "I know you'll pay it back just as soon as you can," she told Mr. Maloney.

"My first paycheck. And ten percent interest," the grateful man promised. "I thank you, kind folks. I thank you again and again. I won't forget this. You'll have a friend if you ever need help." He stood up, started to put his cap on, then took it off and backed out into the kitchen. "Sorry to bother you at dinner. Thanks again, Joe . . . Ma'am."

"Goodnight, Mr. Maloney. Watch your step now on that back walk."

The dinner continued a few minutes in silence, broken only by Dawn's soft humming as she ate her peas, one at a time.

"What's everybody so quiet for?" she asked finally, looking around. "I thought you said it was good news, Daddy."

Joe Wheeler ignored her. "How much is left, Grace? In savings, bonds, everything? . . ."

"About four hundred."

"That's all? My severance pay too?"

"Yes."

Ruth did not realize till Mother began removing the dishes that no one spoke again for the rest of the meal.

As if by mutual consent, scarcely discussing it, Ruth and Kitty stopped going to the movies on Saturdays. The list of things they would need in high school seemed to grow each day. With the money she saved on movies, Ruth could buy a pair of low pumps. So they spent their Saturdays walking or met some of the other girls at the doughnut shop and talked for several hours. Occasionally, if someone could afford a party, they helped celebrate a birthday, or perhaps they would invite the whole crowd over for croquet.

On this particular Saturday, Ruth sat on the edge of the bed, only half-awake, and watched Mr. Maloney leave for his new job downtown. She reached over and raised the window higher. Despite the crisp breeze from the east, the sunshine was warm. She stuck out her legs in the warm patch of sunlight on the floor, enjoying the delight of the spring morning before she started her Saturday chores.

"Do you think we'll have to move, Mother?" Dawn asked as the girls helped clean the high kitchen cupboards. Ruth passed stacks of cups and saucers on to Dawn, who set them on the table, while Mrs. Wheeler attacked the shelves with a soapy sponge.

"Why do you ask that?" Mother said.

"Because Shirley Klaus and her family had to move. They're living in a garage."

"That little girl who always walked to kindergarten with you?"

"Yes. Shirley said the only way they can get in and out is to open the double doors. Shirley says it's so cold she stays in bed most of the time."

"Oh, Lord. The way we have to live these days. Like animals." Mrs. Wheeler stepped down and untied the scarf around her hair.

"Will we have to move?" Dawn repeated, anxious.

"Not if we can meet the mortgage payments," Mother said determinedly, and it was the first time Ruth was conscious of the "if." "If we can scrape together enough each month for that, we'll stay. Thank heavens summer's coming. There will be no coal bills for a while. Summer's the poor man's friend."

"Are we poor?" Dawn asked, surprised.

At first Mother did not answer. Both girls watched her, motionless.

"Oh, not really." Mother dumped out the water in the sink. "But we've sure had our share of bad luck. As soon as Daddy gets a job, things will improve."

It wasn't convincing, somehow.

Dawn stood in the center of the floor thinking it over while Mother went to the window to put up the sign for the ice truck. Ruth sat on a stool to rest. She was struck by Dawn's unselfconscious manner —her lack of awareness that her blouse was too tight across her chest or that her stockings were on wrong side out—of untied shoes and dangling ribbon. Whatever Mother laid out for her the night before, Dawn put on the following morning whether what she wore was in style or not. How simple it would be to be small again till things got better.

"Well, when *is* Daddy going to get a job?" Dawn demanded.

"Your father's a proud man," Mrs. Wheeler answered. "It's not easy."

Perhaps it wasn't pride, Ruth thought. Perhaps it was fear. The fear of trying a different kind of job —of working with different types of people. A fear of not being able to control the situation—of not being able to choose. That was a fear that even she could understand.

Early in the afternoon, Ruth and Kitty went walking. The sharp wind that blew in from the lake had mellowed and sunshine bathed their backs and shoulders. It was a heavenly time to be outside with nothing much to do, and they circled the high school and track. They ambled along the store fronts, skirted the park, and bought a Horton's Dixie Cup, lingering in front of the drug store, watching out of the corners of their eyes for a familiar face.

Whether or not Clyde had ever come by Ruth's, once he had her address, Ruth didn't know. He'd never knocked if he had. But she had seen his own address scribbled on the corner of his notebook. Now the chief activity on Saturday afternoons was an hour's debate with Kitty discussing strategy, followed by a leisurely, well-rehearsed stroll to Clyde's neighborhood, and surveillance from a distance of the house in which he lived. Saturday afternoon was, in short, taken up with the awful hope of being discovered.

57

The first time they went, they merely viewed the house from half a block away. By reading the number on the corner house and counting down, they figured Clyde's house to be a brick duplex with yellow railing around the porch. Slowly they traversed the streets parallel to his, chatting blithely about the doings at school, watching obliquely for any activity in the vicinity of the duplex.

Two Saturdays before, they had dressed in identical sweaters and crisscrossed the end streets. The Saturday after that, on a dare from Kitty, they had crept silently down the alley directly behind Clyde's house, past his very garbage cans, and come out breathlessly again on a side street.

On this particular Saturday, however, with sidewalks warm from the May sun and a softness to the breeze, Ruth decided that this was *it*. They would walk along the sidewalk across the street from Clyde's, in direct view of his front windows. The girls wore their matching sweaters again, thrown carelessly over their shoulders, dusty-rose polish on their nails, despite Mother's disapproval. They were—should they be asked—looking for a short route to the high school from Ruth's house, and were simply testing it out.

It was as though the very air about the street were toxic. Simply turning at Clyde's street sign instead of walking on past as they usually did caused a strange pounding in Ruth's ears, a catch in her breath.

"Relax," Kitty said. "It's a public sidewalk, isn't it?"

"But if he sees us, Kitty, he'll *know!*"

"Know what?"

"That we know where he lives."

"Ruth, if he's watching out that upstairs window he can see us right now," Kitty whispered. "Don't even look toward his house. Keep walking."

Ruth concentrated on looking serene.

"He's only four blocks from the high school," Ruth said. "You know, Kitty, we really could go to school this way."

"Except that we'd have to go an extra three blocks just to get over here," Kitty added, keeping up the chatter.

"Oh, my gosh! Is that someone coming out on the porch?"

"I don't know."

"Please look, Kitty! I couldn't possibly."

"Yes, it is."

"*Clyde?*"

"No. Somebody shaking a rug."

"Oh, God. . . ."

"Ruth, when you get married, don't ask me to stand up for you. If you can't make it down this sidewalk, you'll never make it up the aisle."

A small gray cat jumped out from behind a bush and playfully grabbed at Ruth's ankles. Delighted for the excuse, Ruth swooped the cat up in her arms and sat down on the steps opposite Clyde's to play with it. They took turns dragging a stick through the grass, letting the kitten pounce.

A door opened across the street. Ruth felt the color rising in her cheeks. But when she lifted her eyes, she saw a man come down the steps of the duplex, get in an old model T, and drive off.

After ten minutes, the cat tired of play and settled down in Ruth's lap, purring. The girls began to giggle.

"What do I do now, Kitty?"

"Stay here for the rest of your natural life, I guess."

There were footsteps on the walk behind them, and a somber boy of seven picked up the cat. "That's mine," he said, looking down at them.

"We weren't going to steal it," Kitty told him. "Listen. Does Clyde Heidelberger live around here?"

"Yeah. That's his house right there," the boy said, pointing.

"Oh, Lord, Kitty, don't make him point," Ruth flushed.

"Is he home on Saturdays?"

The boy shrugged. "Why don't you go ask? How should I know?"

"Thanks for nothing," Kitty murmured, standing up.

The boy turned to go inside. Then he added, "I

don't think he is. Sometimes he helps his uncle at the lumberyard on Saturdays."

"Ye gods, Kitty, he's probably not even home," Ruth said, looking directly at the house now. Somehow the magic had dissipated. "Let's go home."

"Stop by the store for some candy," Kitty suggested, and they headed for Lorenzo's without even looking back.

The Italian market was near the Illinois Central tracks, the IC, as the electric railroad was called. The windows in front were always clean. The green awning, torn at one corner, flapped invitingly as the girls entered. Ruth drank in the heady fragrance of onions and apples and potatoes, mingled with the sharp smell of Italian sausage and fennel, big balls of Provolone cheese hanging from the ceiling, and crusty loaves of bread stacked behind the counter. They edged past the customers waiting at the butcher table, and thrust their hands deep in the caramel bin. Ruth chose the white Italian nougats, and her mouth watered as she unwrapped the paper.

Mr. Lorenzo looked up and frowned at Kitty when he saw her. It was his usual greeting, and one, Ruth discovered finally, that had a certain fondness in it. The drooping mouth, the quizzical knotting of the heavy eyebrows, the quick glance of the dark eyes all conveyed a sort of tenderness, and Kitty always responded with a smile and a "Hi, Pop."

"Next Saturday," Kitty told Ruth, getting back to strategy again, "we'll walk by on his side of the street. Maybe we'll go in the evening, when he's just got to be home. And if he still doesn't notice us and come out, we'll go up to the door and ring."

"What would we say? What if Clyde answers?"

"Then we'll tell him we're looking for Etta Page Parkinson, and wonder if he knows where she lives."

"Who's Etta Page Parkinson?"

"I haven't the faintest idea. But doesn't it sound marvelous?"

Ruth took her time going home again, but the moment she entered the hall, she knew something was wrong. Through the French doors of the living room she could see Mrs. Hamilton from next door, one hand to her cheek. And from some corner, hidden from view, she heard Mr. Maloney's voice saying over and over again, "Can't believe it. Just can't believe it."

Dawn noticed Ruth and came out in the hall.

"What's going on?" Ruth whispered.

"Somebody robbed Mr. Maloney."

"Daddy's money?"

Dawn nodded solemnly. "All of it. Mrs. Hamilton's too."

Ruth moved to the door of the living room. She could only see the back of Mr. Maloney's head, the wisp of hair that wouldn't lay flat, the hunched shoulders, the round hands on his knees.

". . . . He looked for all the world like a manager. I swear it!" Mr. Maloney was saying, his voice breaking. "Pressed suit . . . tie. Mr. Lukens. That's what he called himself. 'Never heard of him!' the other operators told me. 'He hired me to run an elevator, starting today. Said he'd have my uniform ready.' And they laughed. Just laughed. 'No Mr. Lukens here,' they said."

"To take advantage of a poor man like that!" said Mrs. Hamilton, her hand still pressed against her cheek.

"They called the police then?" Father asked. His voice sounded tired—more tired than Ruth had ever noticed.

Mr. Maloney nodded. "They said it's the second time it's happened in that building. Happens all the time up and down LaSalle Street and over on Michigan Avenue, they said."

"This man . . . Mr. Lukens . . . he was waiting for you the other day when you brought the fifty dollars?"

"Right there in the lobby. He asked me what size shirt I wore—pants—wrote it all down. Said to be there Saturday at nine, and he'd have the uniform for me. I can't believe it. And you folks' money. I can't get over it."

Ruth went upstairs and lay down on the bed.

63

Wasn't life supposed to be a mixture of good and bad? How did it get all out of balance like this, so that every new thing that came along was something awful? Was it possible to be knocked off your feet so often that finally you just didn't feel like trying any more?

Dawn came in and sat down dejectedly beside her. She wore a flannel shirt and a pair of corduroy pants with straps over the shoulders. There was something so forlorn about the slump of her little back that Ruth reached over and put an arm around her.

"Do you think Daddy will ever get his money back?" Dawn asked, leaning against her.

"Not unless they catch that man before he spends it."

"Is twenty-five dollars a lot of money?"

"It would buy a lot of groceries."

Dawn sighed, and it seemed too grown-up somehow for her, as though a sigh that big shouldn't be coming from a girl so small. Ruth tried to think back to the year when she was in kindergarten. She didn't have such big worries then.

"This is Daddy's problem, sweetie, not yours," she told her. "All you have to do is help Mother and not get into trouble around the house."

It didn't seem to comfort her. The small shoulders remained slumped.

"I forgot to tell you, Ruth," she said. "Somebody called this afternoon."

"Who?"

"I don't know. He didn't say."

"A *boy?*" The pounding began in her ears again.

"Yes."

Ruth pulled away from Dawn and looked at her intently. "What did he say? Can you remember exactly what he said?"

"He said . . . well, I don't really remember. He just wanted to know if Ruth Wheeler was here."

"That's what he called me? Ruth Wheeler? Both names?"

"I think so."

"Dawn, can't you remember anything for sure?"

"Ruth Wheeler. That's what he said." Dawn nodded her head emphatically.

"What did you say?"

"I said you weren't here, of course!"

"Dawn, listen. This is important. What time was it? Can you at least remember that?"

"I can't tell time yet," Dawn whined impatiently, bored with the whole conversation.

"But was it right after I left with Kitty? Or in the middle of the afternoon? Or? . . ."

"It was just before you got home. Just before Mr. Maloney came over."

Ruth fell back on the bed. Clyde must have seen her! He was calling to let her know. He was calling to ask her out. He was calling to say that he couldn't fall for any girl who would chase after a boy like that. He was calling to say he'd been thinking about her a lot. He was calling to say that she looked beautiful sitting across the street in the sun, stroking the cat. He was calling to say she looked stupid stroking the cat. He was calling to say. . . .

"Did he say he'd call back later?" Ruth questioned.

"He just said good-bye."

"What was his voice like? Was it sort of deep—did he talk sort of slow?"

"It was just a *boy*, Ruth! I didn't pay any attention!" Dawn protested, and Ruth grew quiet.

Dawn scooted across the bed and snuggled against her sister again.

"We won't have to live in one, will we, Ruth?" she asked plaintively after a moment.

"What?"

"We won't have to live in a garage like Shirley Klaus, will we?"

"No, of course not," Ruth said, and patted her arm. The worry just wouldn't go away, and Ruth felt it too—more deeply than ever before.

CHAPTER 4

July 28, 1932

Dear Diary:

One more month before high school begins and I still don't have enough money for a pair of pumps. Kitty said that Rose has a pair I could use for the first day, but my feet are wider than hers and I just know they won't fit. I'll be glad when this stupid Depression is over. Father says that Roosevelt will be elected in November if things get much worse. Mother says she doesn't care—that Hoover doesn't deserve another chance. I just wish I could go to sleep for a year and wake up when Dad has a job again.

Ruth stood in the kitchen doorway, her back to her mother, shoulders rigid.

"I'll go tonight, Mother, after it gets dark."

"Ruth Lorraine, I told Mrs. Nesbitt that you girls would be over this afternoon. You can just as easily go one time as another."

"Then I'll go tonight, Mother," Ruth insisted, her face hot.

Mrs. Wheeler snapped a handful of beans in her hand and dropped them into a bowl on her lap. "I can't see what possible difference it makes to you."

Ruth leaned against the doorway and sniffled. "If Clyde . . . or anybody . . . saw Dawn and me carrying laundry home, I'd just die. What would they think?"

"I guess they'd think we were trying as best we could to keep going, Ruth. It's no disgrace what's happening to people now. Everybody's problem is nobody's problem, you know."

"It's *not* everybody's problem!" Ruth turned around, her eyes glistening. "Connie Ebert bought a whole new wardrobe for school. Kitty told me. And even Kitty doesn't have to start high school in an old pair of shoes worn down at the heels."

"I don't know the Eberts," said Mrs. Wheeler,

"but I'd say they're the exception. If it's all so important to you, though, pick up the wash tonight. Just be careful you don't stumble with it in the dark."

Ruth lingered.

"I didn't know things would ever get this bad, Mother."

There was no answer. The silence bothered Ruth more than anything. She tried again.

"How long do you suppose the Depression will last? It'll be over before I'm out of high school, won't it?"

"Sweetheart, things have been hard for us for a long time. Not for everybody, maybe, but for us."

"You never told me."

"For three years, up until the time Grandma Wheeler died, your father and his brothers paid all her doctor bills. And when she was in the hospital out there in Columbus for two months, Daddy paid for it all. 'As soon as we get out from under these medical bills, we'll be okay,' he would say. Well, he hadn't counted on the Depression. Nobody had."

"Why didn't you tell me how bad things really were?"

"There was never any reason to. Why worry little girls with things they can't do anything about?"

"Well, I'm not little now. Is there anything else you haven't told me? I mean, I'll still be able to go to college and everything, won't I?"

Mrs. Wheeler looked up. She started to speak and then stopped, as though her eyes themselves could answer for her. "Honey," she said finally, "I can't even tell you what's going to happen next month, much less three years from now."

It was the first time Ruth had ever even considered the possibility of not going. All her life she'd known she was meant for better things than tapping a typewriter somewhere or selling gloves at Carson, Pirie, Scott. All her life she'd been in the top third of her class, so sure she was going to college. And suddenly she wasn't sure at all.

Tears welled up again and she tried to hide them with her hand, but Mother noticed and reached over to stroke her arm.

"Times are hard, Ruthie, but not hopeless. We'll get by. Your father and I have been through a lot, but we keep going somehow."

Ruth pushed away from the table, the tears rolling now.

"I don't want to just 'keep going,' Mother! I want to *be* something! *Do* something! Just not starving doesn't matter! Just being alive doesn't count!"

Mrs. Wheeler shook her head. "Sometimes it's the *only* thing that matters. Sometimes that and keeping the family together is the most a person can hope for."

"Not for me, Mother. It'll never be enough for me."

Ruth went out on the back porch and sank down in a pile of newspapers in one corner, hidden by boxes and old dressers and other junk that had accumulated year after year. The sun streaming through the windows made her dizzy with the heat, but she leaned against the wall and closed her eyes, wishing she could hide out here forever.

Life wasn't *supposed* to be like this. Life was supposed to reward you if you worked hard. What kind of joke was it to tell her that after she had done so well in school, she might have to forget about college, forget about teaching? Were her dreams so unrealistic? Kitty, of all people, flitted from one idea to another. She used to want to be another Joan Crawford, and lately she'd been talking about being a pilot and flying around with Amelia Earhart! But Ruth had always wanted to teach, as long as she could remember. And now this perfectly sane and sensible dream was coming apart at the seams. Well, she wasn't going to let it. *She wasn't going to let it.*

"I'm not going to let it!" she said suddenly, loudly, getting up and stalking back into the kichen. But the room was empty now, and Ruth was talking to herself.

"You're the Wheeler girls?"

A small lady with fantastically skinny arms opened the door and led the girls into a hallway lighted by a crystal chandelier. Ruth and Dawn followed her through the kitchen and into the pantry.

"It's a pretty big basket. Are you sure you can carry it?"

"Yes," Ruth answered, without expression. She picked up one handle, Dawn the other, and they went back through the hallway, past the antique clock and chairs, and wedged the basket through the front door.

"Tell your mother full starch in the collars and cuffs and light starch in the body, please," Mrs. Nesbitt said pleasantly. "Harold is fussy about his shirts." She smiled, and Ruth hated her. "You know how men are."

There were eleven steps to Mrs. Nesbitt's house, and Ruth's arm ached even before she'd reached the bottom. She had to lean to one side to keep her hand level with Dawn's.

"This is just dumb!" Dawn complained. "We should have come before it got dark! I can't even see the sidewalk!"

"Everyone would see us," Ruth answered tersely.

"So what? What's the matter with a basket of clothes? All the underwear's on the bottom, isn't it?"

Ruth said nothing more. How easy it was when you were only five and didn't care. But at least the family was doing something. At least they were fighting back. That's more than she could say of Annie Scoates.

In her room later, Ruth carefully laid her own clothes out on the bed and looked them over. Three dresses, one with a rip under the sleeve that would require a patch. Another was a blue print that used to be Aunt Marie's and was a little old-fashioned. Only the dotted swiss looked at all good. There were two wool skirts and four blouses, but one didn't go with either skirt. And two sweaters, an old one of Mother's, and the new one that matched Kitty's. Everything else Ruth had outgrown and was waiting in the attic for her sister. Poor Dawn. They would all be out of style when she was ready for them, and by then she would have started to care.

The phone jangled in the hall below just as Ruth was checking her slips and stockings.

"Ruth? Telephone," came her father's voice.

Kitty had gone to Joliet for a few days to visit a married sister and had said she might call. Ruth clattered downstairs and sprawled in the old cane chair by the telephone, her legs stretched out in front of her till her feet reached the opposite baseboard.

"Hi," she said.

There was a momentary pause, and then a new voice, vaguely familiar, said, "Hi."

Ruth bolted up, drawing her heels back so sharply that they hit the legs of the chair.

"This is Clyde," the voice said.

Ruth's heart pounded so hard she felt he surely could hear it.

"Well . . . hi, Clyde!" she said, and was suddenly

embarrassed. What on earth did you say to a boy when he called? There was something so unnatural about talking without seeing the other's face. Was he laughing at her? Serious? It was insanely awkward.

"What'cha doing?"

A sharp giggle escaped from Ruth's throat, and she regretted it. "Just sitting here talking to you. What are you doing?"

"Sitting here talking to you."

They both laughed politely, and fell silent.

"Ready for school?" Clyde asked finally. It sounded as though he were unwrapping a stick of gum and putting it in his mouth.

Ruth began to relax. It was easier now. She could always talk about school. "As ready as I'll ever be, I guess. We probably won't know what books to get till the first day."

"You taking Latin?"

"Yes."

"Going to college, huh?"

"I hope so."

Ruth was conscious of Dawn listening from around the corner. She picked up the telephone, moved it into the hall closet, and shut the door after her.

"What are you doing?" Clyde asked. "Sounds like you're moving the furniture."

"Little pitchers have big ears," Ruth told him. "Escaping from a kid sister, that's all."

"Yeah? You in private now?"

"Sort of. I'm in the closet."

They laughed. This time it was such an easy laugh. Ruth loved the sound of it. She wished they could sound this way forever—that every time she opened her mouth she evoked the same spontaneous reaction from him.

"Listen. I've been hearing strange stories about you," Clyde went on.

"What kind of stories?"

"Well, I heard that you and your tall girl friend tried to steal a neighbor's cat."

"What!"

"That's right. Kid across the street said that a few months ago two girls tried to steal his cat when he wasn't looking and then they asked where I lived. Never did try to steal mine, though."

Ruth burst out laughing. She couldn't help it. But she blushed so hard she could feel the heat from her face against her hand. "We were only playing with his cat," Ruth said. "And it was Kitty who asked where you lived, not me." She felt like a traitor. Would she have said that if Kitty were present? She knew she wouldn't.

"How come Kitty wanted to know?"

Ruth shrugged, then realized he couldn't see it.

"Hey, you still there?" Clyde asked.

"Yes."

"How come Kitty wanted to know where I live?"

"I don't know. Why don't you ask her?"

"Maybe I will. Thought maybe she'd . . . uh . . . like to go to the movies with me."

Ruth blushed again, not knowing how to handle the teasing. "Maybe she would."

"Then again, I don't think she'd do. Have to put on stilts to get up to where I could talk to her. You wouldn't like to go to the movies with me, would you?"

"I might."

"You *might?* Is that all you can say?"

Ruth giggled. "Depends on what's showing."

"Does it matter?"

"No."

"That's what I like to hear. How about Saturday?"

"Okay."

"I'll call you Friday and let you know what time. Okay?"

"Okay."

Ruth emerged from the closet to find her father staring at the cord leading under the closet door.

"What do you call this?" he asked, curious.

"I wanted privacy," Ruth said, feeling foolish as she put the telephone back on the stand. "Dawn was listening."

"I was not!" came the instant reply from around the corner of the living room.

Father sauntered out to the kitchen, his hands in

his pockets. Ruth followed, her eyes dancing, dying to tell someone.

"You know what happened in Washington to-day?" Mr. Wheeler said, staring out the window into the darkness. "MacArthur drove the bonus army out of the capital."

It meant absolutely nothing to Ruth. Her father turned around.

"You know all those jobless vets that marched to Washington to get their pension? They were driven out of the capitol like a pack of rats. My God, I can't believe Hoover let it happen."

Ruth waited, bursting to tell. And finally she could hold it in no longer.

"That was Clyde, Daddy! He's taking me to the movies on Saturday."

Mr. Wheeler looked at Ruth as though he hadn't heard her. Finally his eyes focused on hers. "Clyde who?"

"Heidelberger."

Her father's face softened, and his lips stretched up a little at the corners.

"So that's who you're sweet on, huh? Well, you go have a good time, honey. Make the most of being young. You have a real good time."

The following day, Ruth's father came home from the employment office to say that he had found a job and signed up.

"Oh, Joe! What a relief! I knew this was only temporary." Mrs. Wheeler put down the glass jars which she was dipping in hot water and left the canning for a moment. "What will you be doing? When do you start?" She sat down at the table and wiped her forehead with her apron.

Mr. Wheeler opened the icebox and took out the water jar. "It's nothing special. Acme Company. Engineering firm."

"Engineering?"

"Yeah. Some kind of office job. I'll find out to-morrow." He poured a tall glass of water and drank it without stopping. Ruth went on peeling peaches and watching him. "About ninety again today," he said. "Grace, you ought to stop that canning and get some air. Like a blast furnace in here."

"I can't. Mrs. Hamilton got a bushel of peaches and gave me half. I've got to put them up. They're going soft." Mother opened the neck of her blouse and fanned herself. "Oh, Joe! I'm so glad."

Dawn greeted the announcement of the new job by dancing around the kitchen. The playsuit she was wearing had one broken strap and her braids were half-undone. She looked like an urchin dancing for pennies on Maxwell Street. She grabbed her father's hand and whirled around.

"Okay, okay," Joe Wheeler said, unsmiling. "I didn't say I was going to be congressman, did I?"

"Oh, but to have money coming in again!"

Mother sighed. And she placed a larger order than usual at the store, including a pot roast for dinner that evening.

"Seems like old times, Mrs. Wheeler," the deliveryman said as he cheerfully set the box on the table amid the jars of warm peaches.

"Mr. Wheeler's working again," Mother said simply, getting the money from her purse.

"Know you're glad about that. Give the mister my regards."

It was a good dinner that evening, with meat and potatoes, green beans, and a fresh peach cobbler. Father seemed in no hurry to leave the table, and stayed there talking with Mother long after Dawn had gone outside to play and Ruth had gone to her room.

Ruth opened both of her windows wide to catch the cross breeze and lay down on the cool floor. Her stomach was full, and the house was filled with good familiar sounds again—the tinkle of dishes in the kitchen, Father's low voice, Dawn's laughter from somewhere outside. They were friendly sounds, secure sounds, like maybe the worst was over. She decided to casually tell Clyde about Father's new job. She wouldn't even have to mention Smythes.

Clyde, I'd like you to meet my father. He's with Acme Engineering now.

No, that didn't sound right. She'd have to wait

till Clyde asked. Did boys ever ask where your father worked, she wondered. How had she managed to tell him that Father worked for Smythes? She couldn't remember.

Downstairs, the screen door slammed.

"Ruth, Kitty's here!" Dawn bellowed.

"Kitty!"

There were hurried footsteps on the stairs and the girls fairly flew at each other. Ruth pulled her into the bedroom and leaned breathlessly against the door.

"He called."

"Who?" Kitty asked.

It was the moment for which Ruth had been waiting, and yet Kitty had had to ask who. "Who else?"

Kitty curled up on the bed, drawing her legs up beneath her. "What did he say? Tell me everything!"

Ruth tried to remember the way he sounded when he said hi, the way it surprised her, the way they laughed, and how she had taken the phone in the closet. Each new bit of information brought exclamations and giggles from Kitty. It was like getting the phone call all over again.

"And Kitty, guess what!"

"What?"

"He knew about us walking down his street and about the little boy's cat. The boy told Clyde we asked where he lived and that we tried to steal his cat!"

Kitty shrieked. "What did you say?"

"I didn't know what to say, Kitty. I was so embarrassed. Finally I . . . oh, Kitty, I said you were the one who asked."

Kitty shrieked again and fell back on the bed. "Ruth, you didn't!"

"Kitty, I had to say *something!* He knew. He asked!"

Kitty sat up again, eager to hear more. "What did he say?"

"He wanted to know why you wanted to know."

"What did you say?"

"I told him he'd have to ask you."

"What did *he* say?"

"He said maybe he would."

Kitty collapsed again, moaning. "Did he say anything else about me?"

Instantly Ruth remembered Clyde's remark about Kitty's height. "No," she said. "That was all."

There was a thud against the wall and a soft "Ow!"

"That's Dawn again!" Ruth stormed out to the hall and into Charles's room. Dawn was crouched by the closet, rubbing her knee, and an overturned box had spilled clothes out over the floor.

"For heaven's sake, Dawn, will you quit eavesdropping in that closet?" Ruth snapped. "Can't you find anything else to do but spy on us?"

"Ow!" Dawn was whispering to herself, trying to divert the attention to her knee.

"Go have Mother put some salve on it," Ruth said. "And if I find you in here again, I'm going to tell her you've been climbing all over Charles's stuff, trying to hear us through the wall."

Dawn limped downstairs, and Ruth bent over to pick up the little shoes and shirts and put them back in the box.

"You mean your mother still keeps these?" Kitty asked incredulously, kneeling down to help.

Ruth nodded. "She wouldn't give them away for anything. She kept all his toys, too—the closet's full of his stuff. And you know what? When Aunt Marie came to visit us last summer, she had to sleep on the daybed in the dining room. Mother didn't even let her sleep in Charles's room."

"Creepy," said Kitty.

"Not to Mother."

They slid the box back in the closet and went to Ruth's room again.

"I haven't told you the best, Kitty. He's taking me to the movies on Saturday."

"Oh, Ruth! What will you wear?"

"My dotted swiss. It's all I've got."

"Then you've just got to wear Vera's belt with it. She has one embroidered with little green and white flowers. It would be fabulous."

"It's my shoes, though, Kitty. They're awful!"

"I'll bring Rose's pumps over tomorrow, and you can walk around in them."

"Oh, Kitty! I wish you were going with me! I feel so embarrassed. What if he takes me out for something to eat afterwards? What will I order?"

"I'll ask Rose. She'll know."

"And then, when he brings me *home,* Kitty! That's the worst part! What do I do? Do I ask him in? Should I sit out on the porch and talk? What will I say? Am I supposed to go in first or wait till he says he has to go? Oh, God, Kitty, I didn't realize it would be like this. I won't have any fun at all!"

Kitty thought it over. "I could arrange to be sitting on the front porch when you got back. And then you could ask him to walk me home, and on the way I'd find out what he really thinks of you and everything."

"Oh, Kitty, would you? That would be perfect!"

Kitty thought some more. "No. That wouldn't work. Then *I'd* be stuck with saying good-night."

Ruth threw herself on the bed and lay like a zombie. "Kitty, do you think we'll ever get married? I just didn't know it would be so awful!"

The figures on the large screen moved and spoke and blinked their eyes, but Ruth was conscious only of the feel of Clyde's hand around hers. Halfway through the picture, as casually as anyone could imagine, he had gently lifted Ruth's arm, slipping his own underneath, and clasped her hand in his. Neither looked at the other. Each sat with his eyes fixed straight ahead, but for a moment Ruth had stopped breathing. The intimacy of it all, flesh against flesh, the warmth of Clyde's palm, made her feel as though the hands themselves were two conscious entities, communicating with each other there in the darknesss between the seats. She swallowed and was sure that he heard it.

For a while, Ruth felt that if nothing else good ever happened to her, this one moment would make up for everything. It was perfect, for she didn't have to worry about what to say or what to do. She didn't even have to look at him—just sit there and let it happen. Their fingers had locked as though they were parts in a puzzle, made for each other.

It was strange how little she had actually noticed about him before. All the time they were merely flirting with each other in the halls at school, she had been careful not to observe him too closely, not to let him catch her looking at him.

Now that he had asked her out, however, and the attraction was official, it seemed permissible to look at him directly when he spoke to her, to study him when he stopped outside the theater to look at the posters, to notice the way he sat with his fingers interlaced, his legs crossed with the ankle of one over the knee of the other—just like her father sat, she thought approvingly.

He was even more handsome than she remembered, dressed in a checked suit and blue tie with a handkerchief, even, in the pocket. His hair was light brown, but his eyes were dark, like two ripe olives, and it was this contrast, Ruth decided, that made him so attractive. They seemed to fit perfectly a face with a cleft in the chin. Clyde had a way of smiling with his eyes, not his mouth, and Ruth found it necessary, when he talked, to watch his eyes to know when he was teasing.

She did not want this moment to end, ever. She did not want to have to cram her feet back into the tight shoes Rose had lent her or worry about what was coming next. She wanted to sit out her four years of high school just like this, with her hand in Clyde's.

The lights came on, however, and Clyde's fingers untwined from between hers and disappeared.

"Like it?" he asked.

She nodded. "Great."

There were times when Ruth believed that Chicago, on a summer evening, must be paradise. This evening was one of them. Whenever they reached a corner, the breeze from the lake, two miles away, caressed their faces.

"Hungry?" Clyde asked as they neared the drugstore.

"Oh, sort of," Ruth hedged. "I'll bet you are."

"I'm always hungry."

He opened the door for her, and they walked to the long marble counter along one side.

Ruth perched daintily on one of the high stools, letting the shoes slide off the back of her heels where blisters were forming, glad for the relief. She asked for a dish of chocolate ice cream, and Clyde ordered a pineapple sundae for himself. They talked as they ate, discussing the picture show, watching each other's reflections in the mirror behind the counter.

When two boys from school came into the store, Ruth was drunk with the delight of being seen. She was Clyde's girl for the evening, and knew it would get around.

"Hi, Clyde, how you doin'?" one said as they passed, looking carefully at Ruth, and she smiled as she savored the ice cream in her spoon.

The biggest thrill of all, however, came as Ruth and Clyde left the drugstore and started across the street. At the same moment, Connie Ebert and two of her friends were crossing from the other side, and Ruth could see the girls staring at her as they approached.

"Hi, Clyde," Connie said, raising her eyebrows in what Ruth felt was a very affected smile.

"Hi, Connie."

"Who's he *with*?" Ruth heard someone whisper

to Connie after the girls had passed, and she couldn't wait to tell Kitty about this marvelous bit of luck. Now the news would really travel.

The street lights shone all shimmery through the leaves overhead, making soft shadows on the sidewalk. One stretch was particularly dark, and Clyde put his arm around her briefly as they walked, dropping it again when they reached the corner.

Finally Ruth found herself standing on the bottom step of her porch, Clyde on the sidewalk below, her face slightly higher than his. Her heart pounded wildly, and panic replaced all the good feelings she'd had before. She felt almost sick. It was awful standing there like that, not knowing whether she should turn and go in or stay. There was nothing quite appropriate to do with her hands. She fumbled awkwardly with her purse, feeling like a scarecrow. Why on earth had she moved up on the step? Now she was taller than Clyde, and if he tried to kiss her it would be just awful. She couldn't step back down now as though she expected it. . . .

"Well," she sighed.

"Well, guess it's time for me to go," Clyde said.

"It was a marvelous evening, Clyde. I really had a good time."

It sounded so polite, so rehearsed, that Ruth wanted to take it all back and try again. But somehow it must have sounded right to Clyde, because his eyes smiled up at her, and he reached out and tweaked her chin.

"You're a funny little mouse," he said. "I had a good time, too."

And then he was walking away, stopping at the end of the walk to wave briefly, then disappearing in the shadows in his beautiful checked suit.

Ruth went inside, closing the screen softly. Her parents were in the living room listening to the radio. She did not want to talk with anyone right now. She crept on by them and went up to her room.

Taking off Rose's shoes for the last time, she lay down on her bed and smiled up at the darkness. Later on, she knew, she would call Kitty and they would go over every minute of the evening. Later on she would lie in bed and relive everything he had said and wonder if he really liked her and what he meant by "little mouse." But right now she did not want to break the spell. Slowly one hand grasped the other, her fingers interlaced, and she lay there, remembering.

CHAPTER 5

November 9, 1932

Dear Diary:

Roosevelt won the election yesterday. Mother told me at breakfast. Miss Harley had it written on the blackboard when we got to school. I passed some people singing "Happy Days Are Here Again." They must have been Democrats. Now I will have to get used to saying President Roosevelt instead of President Hoover. Father says he doesn't see how a smart-aleck governor from New York is going to do anything Hoover couldn't do, but he voted Democratic anyway for the first time in his life. Mother did too. People say that the Depression will turn the corner now and things will get better, but Mother worries all the time. She won't even spend money to go to the dentist, and two of her teeth are turning dark.

Kitty likes Ted Engles on the basketball team, but he hardly knows she exists.

Ruth's footsteps echoed along the hallway, answering the staccato sound of her mother's heels in the bare rooms.

"Did you ever see such a big bath!" Ruth called. "There's room for two big vanities!"

Mrs. Wheeler came across the hall and looked in. "Why, I never!" She walked on inside and stared, brushing at the wispy strands of hair that floated about her face. "And look at all the shelves for towels!"

"This could be my room!" Dawn's voice rang out from the end of the hall. "Look, Mother! I could climb right out on the porch roof if I wanted!"

"And the closets!" Mrs. Wheeler opened a door in the bedroom at the end of the hall to find a built-in chest of drawers at the back. "Couldn't we use this storage space, though!"

"I'd want the room with the blue flowered wallpaper," Ruth put in, just in case.

Mother started back downstairs. "I wonder what your father thinks of the basement. Eleven rooms in a house, and the first thing a man will look at is the basement. Of course, the sink would have to be replaced in the kitchen, and that paper in the living room is terrible. . . ."

But Joe Wheeler hadn't looked at the basement. He stood in the hallway below, hat in hand.

"You don't like it," Mother said at once, disappointed.

"No point to it, Grace," he said impatiently. "No sense looking at other houses when we're worried about keeping the one we've got."

"I know. I don't mean we'd buy one now, but if things *did* get better . . ."

Father shrugged and reached for the doorknob. "Roof leaks. Comes through the corner bedroom and all down one side of the dining room. You can see the water stains. All you'd be doing, Grace, is exchanging one set of problems for another."

Mother sighed and took one last look at the kitchen. "It's such a pretty window overlooking the backyard," she mused. "All that garden space out there—I could have gladiolus and rose bushes too!"

Father was already walking to the car, and the girls followed silently.

It was all a game, Ruth decided as she climbed in the back seat and took her turn at holding the door closed. For three years they had gone to see every house that was for sale in the area, especially those with garden space. Ruth used to be alarmed that they might actually leave the neighborhood. As the months went by, however, she realized that Sunday afternoon house hunting was free entertainment for Mother, nothing more. Father was growing weary of it, however, burdened with problems that were all too real. And so they drove back home to wait for the New Deal that Roosevelt had promised. But winter was yet to come, and the March inauguration a long way off.

Miss Harley had a perfectly oval face, with large blue eyes and light brown hair that fell in a gentle wave over one side of her face. She wore soft wool dresses that hung from her slim body in graceful folds like the sculptured garments on Greek statues. She was the type of woman that the boys tended to protect and the girls to imitate. And when she stood at the front of the class, reading selections from Edith Wharton or Thomas Wolfe, her vibrant voice captured the attention of the entire room, and Ruth knew that this was the teacher she'd dreamed of being, a teacher who could electrify her students by sheer drama and enthusiasm.

It had been rumored that Miss Harley had gone to Broadway as an actress but had had a nervous breakdown, and returned to Chicago to teach. It was rumored that Miss Harley's older brother had been killed in the World War and that she herself had almost died of grief. It was said that her lover was tubercular, and they had promised never to marry anyone else. All kinds of things were whispered about Miss Harley, but they only added to the mystique.

Up until now, English had been awkward boys mumbling poetry by James Whitcomb Riley or Kipling to the rest of the class. It had meant memorizing long selections from "Thanatopsis" and "Lochinvar." It had meant fidgeting in seats while uninspired teachers with nasal voices had tried to read "The Legend of Sleepy Hollow" with expression, to make Edgar Allan Poe sound scary. And the more they tried, the deadlier the words became when they were released upon the class.

But now the words had a kind of magic about them for Ruth. Now the little black marks on paper seemed of themselves possessed by the spirits that haunted Miss Harley's blue eyes, and if she stood in the front of the room and declared that she was the fair Ophelia, then by the grace of Shakespeare himself, the fair Ophelia she was.

But she was not always sober. If a story amused her, she would stop in the middle of the reading and laugh along with the others. She approached each selection as though she herself had never seen it before, caught up along with the others with the wonder of the words.

Once, when she was in the middle of a scene from *Antony and Cleopatra*—in which a messenger arrives to announce that Antony has married someone else—Miss Harley, as Cleopatra, was about to begin her rage when a boy was sent up from the office with the daily attendance forms. Without breaking character for a moment, Miss Harley took the papers he handed her and shrieked:

> What say you? Hence,
> Horrible villain! or I'll spurn thine eyes
> Like balls before me; I'll unhair thy head:
> Thou shalt be whipp'd with wire, and
> stew'd in brine,
> Smarting in lingering pickle.

And then, as the wide-eyed boy bolted quickly for the door to the laughter of the class, Miss Harley stopped reading long enough to thank him for helping her make the scene more convincing. This thoughtfulness, in the very midst of drama, won her over forever as Ruth's teacher of teachers, and sealed her desire to steep herself in the magic of language and all its emotions.

"I want to teach, Miss Harley," Ruth confided once after class as she helped collect test papers.

Miss Harley brightened and looked at her intently for a moment. "I think you'd be very good at it, Ruth," she said. "I really do."

The pact was complete. It was as though Ruth

had signed her soul away. She had given her life to Miss Harley, and nothing could stop her now.

For two days, the outdoor temperature hovered at sixty degrees, as though defying November. Sitting on the wall surrounding the high school, her back against a warm concrete pillar, Ruth stretched her legs out in front of her and turned her face up to the sun. She couldn't think of a better way to celebrate her fifteenth birthday.

She knew that Clyde was watching her, and when she opened her eyes again, he was smiling. They sat facing each other, and as their feet touched, he tapped a rhythm on the soles of her shoes with his own. He looked suave and much older, somehow, propped lazily up on the wall, arms folded across his chest.

"What are you thinking?" he asked her.

She shrugged and laughed a little. "What are you?"

"I asked first."

Ruth closed her eyes again. "I was wondering what you'd do if I moved away." She was testing him, and felt both nervous and daring.

"Where to?"

"I don't know. Out of the neighborhood somewhere."

He thought for a minute. "I guess I'd ask for your new address."

Ruth laughed.

"Well, are you really moving?" Clyde questioned.

"I don't know. Probably not. Every so often Mother gets the urge, and we go looking at houses."

"I can go pretty far on a bike," Clyde said humorously, and then—dramatically—"I'd climb the highest mountain, swim the deepest ocean, crawl over the desert on my hands and knees. . . ."

That didn't really answer Ruth's wonderings.

"Would you go as far as Chicago Heights or Joliet?"

"I'd hitchhike down," Clyde said, eyes twinkling, ". . . say, once a year or so."

Ruth frowned indignantly. "If that's all you bothered to come, you might find me married."

Clyde grinned. "Fancy that! I'd come down and find you'd turned into a fat little housewife with seven kids."

"Not me. I'm going to be a teacher. You wouldn't find me fat, either."

Clyde put his hands behind his head, grinning broadly, ignoring what she'd said. "Seven kids, fat, and an eighth on the way," he teased.

Ruth started to reply, but suddenly her eye caught sight of a familiar car across the street at the gas station. As she watched, her father got out, waved to a man inside, and started around to the rest room at the back, carrying a burlap sack.

Ruth stared. He was not dressed as she had seen

96

him that morning in his suit and tie. Instead, he was wearing a gray work shirt, soiled blue overalls, and work shoes caked with mud. Ruth squinted as though her eyes were not in focus. Had he changed jobs without telling her?

"Hey," Clyde said, giving her feet another tap. "Why so quiet?"

Ruth tried to remember what they'd been talking about.

"You mad or something? Because I said you'd be fat?"

Ruth smiled, but did not take her eyes off the gas station. "No. You'll be fat and paunchy before I will."

"Let's bet on it," said Clyde. "If you move away, I'll look you up in ten years and find out."

"It's a deal," Ruth told him.

When Mr. Wheeler appeared again, he was dressed in the suit and tie he had worn that morning, and again he carried the sack. He opened the trunk, put the bag inside, and drove away.

Ruth sat motionless, saying nothing. What did it mean? He was only six blocks from home. Why change here? She felt she had witnessed something she wasn't supposed to see, something that Dad had taken great pains to conceal all these months. Did Mother know, she wondered? Yes, she must. But the neighbors didn't. This whole charade—how important it must be to him.

Your father is a proud man, Mother had said once, and Ruth knew now what she meant. The Depression made people secretive.

"Clyde," she ventured, "did you ever hear of a company called Acme?"

"Over near Halsted?"

"I think so."

"Yeah. What about it?"

"Is it an engineering company or what?"

"Heck no. Demolition. Tears down old buildings and stuff. Had a cousin who used to work there. Why? You looking for a job? Hey, you'd be great at it! Hurricane Ruth!"

She gave his feet a kick, and was glad he let the subject drop. She'd never say any more to him about Father—ever.

It didn't really matter. Just before Christmas, Father was laid off, and all his pretenses about working for an engineering firm were irrelevant. The house was cold, and the laundry was done in water that was merely warm. Mother refused to use the mortgage money to buy fuel. The coal in the basement was used sparingly.

"Put on another sweater," she said sharply when Ruth complained.

It was the worst Christmas Ruth ever remembered, yet somehow that didn't seem important either. The biggest concern was about what hadn't happened yet, what might be coming next.

Dawn, however, felt disappointed when she came downstairs that morning and found only an orange and a few walnuts in her stocking. But later, when she opened a box of doll clothes, made from left-over sewing scraps, she was elated, and threw her arms around her mother declaring, "This is the *best* Christmas!"

A relative had sent the Wheelers a smoked sau-sage. This was Christmas dinner, and Joe Wheeler was ashamed. He sat on the edge of the davenport, arms on his knees, and watched somewhat distract-edly while Dawn dressed her doll in new outfits and showed them to him one at a time.

"Very nice," he murmured, and the tired lines on his face formed a patent smile.

Pinned to the wallpaper in the dining room were the colored Christmas pictures of the Madonna and child that Mother had cut from magazines and saved over the years. Ruth sat on the day bed with Dawn and looked at them, remembering the famil-iar details of *Adoration of the Magi* from Christ-mases past, trying to see them through Dawn's won-dering eyes. The great thing about being small was that you didn't know very much about trouble. You assumed that whatever happened, your parents would work it out. It wasn't always true. There was nothing they could do about the Depression, they said, but wait, and that was infinitely more difficult than Ruth had ever imagined. In fact, she didn't believe it. That was giving up, and if she did that, she might as well forget about college forever.

Clyde came over briefly on Christmas afternoon and gave Ruth a bottle of cologne. Kitty was there at the time, so the three of them went for a walk along the cold Chicago sidewalks.

It had evidently not been a good Christmas for Kitty either. Most of the time Ruth thought of her as sweet and even-tempered, but this day there was a sharpness to her voice that was unmistakable.

"Every time I see those pictures of debutantes in their gorgeous dresses it mades me furious," she said. "Their fathers spend thousands just for one party! I think instead of 'coming out' they should be shut away until the Depression's over. It really takes nerve to put a picture like that in the paper when everyone else is so poor."

It was an awkward afternoon, not at all the kind of Christmas Ruth read about where young lovers turned their faces up toward the sky to catch the snowflakes, or snuggled against each other by a fire. For a while after Clyde left, Ruth was terrified that she might even have forgotten to thank him for the cologne, but Kitty said she was sure she had. The sooner the holidays were over, Ruth thought, the better. She wanted to get back to the plain old humdrum days when no one particularly expected to be happy.

Father did not lie on the couch any longer now.

Being out of work was not the shock it had been the first time around, and he prowled through the house like a cat, the worry etched on his face. Sometimes he went next door to talk to Mr. Maloney. The two sat out on the side steps of Mrs. Hamilton's house so Maloney could smoke his cigar. They had a way of talking without ever looking at each other, both staring over the frozen ground, leaning backwards, collars turned up and hands in their coat pockets.

As the days went by, the worry became more intense. There was no money now for gasoline, so the car was put up on blocks. Father's nervousness took on a desperate quality that gave his eyes a haunted look. When Ruth spoke to him, she felt he was not really seeing her.

Sitting near the radio one evening, listening to Fannie Brice as the impossible Baby Snooks, Ruth was distracted by an argument in the dining room.

"I *didn't* accuse you of not trying," Mrs. Wheeler was saying. "I just don't understand how we got to be in this situation. I would think that a man who's been in business for nineteen years would have made *some* contacts *somewhere*. Think of all the people you've done favors for. I can't believe that not one of them couldn't help you if he just knew how things are with us. It's pride, that's the problem! Afraid somebody will see you looking down and out. . . ."

No one was quite prepared for what happened next. Joe Wheeler leaped from his chair where he had been filling out forms and hurled the pencil across the room at the buffet.

"Joe!" Mother half turned, staring.

Ruth did not move. She felt she could not even breathe. Without a word, Mr. Wheeler strode from the room and started down the stairs to the basement, his feet hitting each step with a sharp thud.

Ruth focused on the wall ahead of her, afraid to look at her mother, pretending she hadn't seen. When she finally turned her eyes to the dining room, Mrs. Wheeler was standing in the doorway, one hand at her throat, like a marble statue.

And then Ruth heard the sound of the coal shovel scraping the cement floor of the basement—the clink of metal against the furnace door and the faraway sound of coal falling into the furnace. Again the shovel scraped and the metal clunked and the coal fell, and again and again. Mrs. Wheeler winced, pressing her lips hard together. Three, four, five, six unheard-of shovelfuls of coal. And then the scraping stopped. The house was warm again for the first time that winter.

As the days went on, Ruth felt an empathy with her mother that she had not recognized before. It was the helplessness that was so awful, and Ruth felt it too. While Father made the rounds of stores and offices and employment centers, Mother could only guess what he was doing, and it never seemed enough.

Like an elderly woman with pain in the joints, she harped at him continually and found fault. He did not get out early enough, she said; any man who was serious about a job would be out on the street at seven in the morning. She did not think he wore appropriate clothes for interviews, did not check with the employment office enough, did not take her suggestions about going to see influential people who might be able to help. Ruth cringed at the way her mother went on about it, and still she felt the helplessness of sitting at home, waiting and not knowing. Dawn, in her own way, sensed the tension too, and reacted by whining and crying more than usual, upsetting the household still further.

A silence began to grow between them—Joe Wheeler and his wife. Conversation was limited to necessary remarks. But Ruth did not really know just how desperate the financial situation had become until one evening in the middle of January.

Mother was dishing out a pan of cooked beans and salt pork. Without looking at anyone, she laid the spoon beside the serving dish and said, "I'm going to put a 'room for rent' sign in the window this week."

The announcement was greeted with complete silence.

"Charles's room?" Ruth said at last. "You mean somebody's going to live in it?"

"Yes." Mother sat down and unfolded her napkin. Her sweater was soiled and torn, but there was a damask napkin on her lap as always. "It will just be till things get better. Then . . . we'll see."

Father was strangely gentle. He watched her as she picked up her fork and toyed with the food. "Might be a good idea, Grace—renting it out—if anybody'll take it. Know you've been hating to do it, though."

Mother's lower lip trembled, but she held her head rigid. "It's a question of saving the memory of a dead child at the expense of two who are living," she said.

"That's not going to keep me from remembering," Father said, trying to reassure her. "We've still got all his things."

"Those are going, too." Mother spoke quickly, as though afraid she might change her mind. "I was thinking about it all last week. Annie Scoates's newest baby could use them . . . all the little shirts and coats and things . . . he might as well h-have them. . . ." Mother gulped, and this time she did not fight the single tear that rolled down her cheek. "The material will go to pieces if it's not used. Ruth, I want you to help me carry them over on Saturday. I can't afford train fare for all three of us, so Dawn can stay home this time."

Mother was braver than Ruth had thought— braver than any of them had imagined. Life had been more unfair to her perhaps than to anyone else.

It had dashed her dream of having a greenhouse and flowers, taken her only son while he was still small. And now, in a final cruelty, it was robbing her even of her keepsakes. Still, Mother fought back. As long as she had daughters left, she wasn't giving up.

For several days Ruth returned from school to find her mother in Charles's room. Sometimes she sat down with her and helped, surprised at the rapidity with which her mother worked—the fast decisions about what to save and what to throw away.

His first sweater and cap, Mother saved—also his booties and drinking cup. These went into a box, which Mother held on her lap as tenderly as though she were holding Charles himself. She did not talk much, handing things to Ruth to be folded and put in the sack for Annie, or thrown into the waste basket if they were disintegrating. Only once did Mother's feelings come out, when she picked up the cloth puppy that Charles had always taken to bed with him. Suddenly she pressed it against her chest and cried noiselessly, her mouth open, her face wet.

And then it was over. The puppy went into the keepsake box and the sorting continued. The next day a sign went up in the living room window, "Room for Rent," and the iceman was asked to pass the word around.

Things seemed to have improved somewhat between Ruth's parents. The very fact that there was a "room for rent" sign in the window made them all feel that they were doing *something*. It was a feeling that Ruth found essential.

For a while the only money coming in had been the three dollars that Mrs. Wheeler earned a week washing and ironing for Mrs. Nesbitt. It was the sacrifice of Charles's room, however, that prompted Ruth's father to take any job at all; and so he went from house to house selling matches and shoelaces, the only job he could find. On Saturdays he sometimes demonstrated potato peelers or meat grinders in store windows, and Ruth died a thousand deaths when she thought about it. But the humiliation was slowly replaced by a kind of grim determination, and the worse things were, the angrier and bolder Ruth became. She carried Mrs. Nesbitt's laundry now in broad daylight without complaint. She didn't like it, but she accepted it with a fierce pride, like the sneer on the face of the girl in Hooverville. Despite all their efforts, however, they rarely earned more than fifteen dollars per week, and money for the mortgage, which came out of savings, was almost gone. Keeping the house had become the focal point of all their hopes, as though this, somehow, would see them through.

On Saturday, Ruth and her mother took the IC again to Hazel Crest and began the long walk to the east side of the town where the poorest residents lived. Halfway there, the milk wagon offered to take them the rest of the way for a nickel, but Mother refused. There wasn't a penny to spare.

Wisps of Mrs. Wheeler's reddish hair fanned out from beneath her felt hat, and her skirt blew straight backwards as the force of the wind hit them squarely. Once, when Mother lifted her feet, Ruth noticed that one of her shoes was splitting at the seam. It was the only pair her mother owned. In fact, it was the only pair Ruth remembered her mother wearing, except for a white pair in summer and some slippers on Sunday morning. For at least six years they had been far more impoverished than Ruth had ever imagined. What a sacrifice those birthday dresses must have been, and Ruth had accepted them as though they were her right. Her face burned, and a wave of panic swept over her. They were "poor folks"—poor, poor, poor! Why hadn't she realized this before? Anybody could tell just by looking! Yet they continued in the same house, next door to the comfortable home of Mrs. Hamilton, as though nothing had happened. Ruth was appalled at the discovery. They couldn't let things get worse.

She was still thinking about it when they reached Annie Scoates's front yard. The door to the dirty white shack was tightly closed, and the windows had been covered up with newspaper to keep out the cold. Only the smoke that poured through the chimney told them that someone was home.

Mother set her bag on the doorstep and knocked. There was no sound from inside, as though all the inmates were hibernating here in the hovel, waiting for spring. Then the handle turned, and the door opened a mere crack. Ruth could see a human eye peering at them and the odor of stale clothes instantly filled her nostrils, as though the eye itself were contaminated with the smell.

Then suddenly the door opened wide, and Annie Scoates stood there in a dress with its sleeves removed, her arms thrust in a dirty sweater that she wore underneath it.

"Lord! Miz Wheeler! And Ruthie! Well, I never! Come on in!" She closed the door after them and clasped Mrs. Wheeler's hands in hers. "And here I am lookin' like this. Haven't even tended my hair."

Her face was even more wrinkled than Ruth remembered, and it seemed strange somehow because her hair was still blond.

"How have you been, Annie?" Mother said, squeezing her arm. "And the children?"

Like a frightened rabbit, Timothy Scoates jumped up from the table where he was eating a piece of bread and lard, and stood with his back against the wall, hugely embarrassed. Ruth noticed that the socks above his shoes were no socks at all, but merely cutoffs from the bottoms of long underwear, worn around the ankles to give the appearance of stockings. There was a space between the bottom of his knickers and the top of the "socks," and then another expanse of skin between the cutoffs and the shoes. He knew that Ruth was staring at his feet and blushed fiercely.

"Well, we're hangin' on," Annie said, and pointed to the twins who were peeping out from the other room. "Polly and Jeanette have got the chicken pox, wouldn't you know. Here now, you girls, get back in bed."

Ruth tried not to look at the sores on their faces, but was drawn to them in revulsion. The baby, nearly a year old now, pulled himself up on wobbly legs and stood clinging to a chair, staring at the visitors. Ruth tried to imagine him in Charles's clothes.

"Oh, it's *so* good to see you!" Annie continued, offering Mrs. Wheeler and Ruth seats near the table, which sent Timothy scurrying out of the room altogether, his bread left behind. "Weather gits bad like this, seems I don't get out of the house hardly at all. How's Dawn? You didn't bring her? And the husband?"

"We're in good health, thank goodness," Mother said. "But Joe lost his job. After nineteen years. . . ."

"Oh, Miz Wheeler!"

"He's selling shoelaces now, Annie, door-to-door. I never thought I'd see the day. That's all he can find. Heaven only knows where it will end."

Feeling less shy now, the baby edged more boldly toward Ruth, its nose running. She fixed her eyes on him sternly. He paused, grinned up at her, and came on. Ruth shook her head at him. *No,* she thought. *Go somewhere else.* He grunted and took another step forward, hitting at her playfully with one hand. His palm was sticky, and Ruth drew back to get out of his reach. As she pulled her knee away, the baby lost his balance and fell down. Instantly he began to howl, and Ruth was mortified.

What kind of person was she, anyway? What had this small baby to do with the Depression? Was it his fault that his face was dirty? He could do no more about his condition than the Wheelers could do about theirs. They were all in this together, and the thought sickened her.

Annie picked the baby up and held him to her, not noticing what had happened. The crying stopped.

"It's that way all over, Miz Wheeler," Annie was saying, "and nothin' to be ashamed of. We're all in the same boat, travelin' the same river. God's truth."

Mother took a deep breath. "I'm renting out Charles's room, Annie, and I b . . . brought his things for Benjamin."

Ruth was surprised at what happened next. Annie Scoates simply reached forward and took Mother's hands in her own, and the two women began to cry together softly, tears running down their faces.

Finally Annie said, in a hoarse whisper, "I used to wash his little arms. He'd get so dirty out there by the side of the house," and Mother nodded quickly, remembering. "Bless you, Miz Wheeler. I know how hard it is for you to give 'em away."

Mother bit her lip, trying to stop the tears. Ruth watched her uncomfortably. There was a kind of empathy between Mother and Annie Scoates that made her feel left out.

"There are all sorts of little trousers and shirts and sweaters," Mother said, more in control now. "We tucked some toys in, too. I wanted Benjamin to have them. You kn . . . knew Charles too, Annie, and loved him like we did."

"God's truth," Annie said again.

The women parted from each other, wiped their faces, and withdrew into themselves. Benjamin had crawled down from his mother's lap now and was making his way along the wall, holding onto the few pieces of furniture.

"Who took the room?" Annie asked.

"No one yet. I've put a sign in the window, and the iceman has been passing the word along."

Annie shook her head. "Charles's room," she said sadly. "The Depression changes things . . . changes people, don't it? I've seen good boys—boys like my Timothy—turn into coyotes. Steal clothes off the line, they will—milk off of porches. When you see a boy doin' somethin' like that, that's how he is, you see? But tomorrow he can be different. We're all of us different, according to what's happening to us. I swear, Miz Wheeler, if it came to that, I could steal bread from a store for my babies! Yes I could! I don't like to think on it, but I know I would if I had to."

Annie stopped and leaned back in her chair reflectively, her bony arms folded across her chest. "Problems didn't use to seem so bad when I was younger. Never had nothin' more'n I do now, but I was movin' about from place to place. When you're movin' on, you never stop long enough for trouble to catch up with you. But when you settles somewhere, the trouble man knows where you're at."

"If we just *knew* things were going to get better sometime, even if we didn't know when, it would be easier," Mother said. "It's the not knowing—the worrying that maybe things will get even worse—that's hardest."

"Most valuable thing to lose is hope," Annie commented. "A man can take a lot if he has hope, but if you take that away, he's got nothin'." She shook her head again, as though trying to shake off the memories. "The things I've seen." She turned her face sideways and hid her mouth in her hand, head tucked down, chin trembling. "Baby up the road, mama puts salt pork gravy in its bottle. No milk.

The mama's all dried up. Little thing cries half the night. I got hardly enough for my Benjamin any more or I'd nurse him myself. And boys turned out from home these days to get work earlier and earlier. Thirteen, fourteen . . . they turn 'em out. Kids afraid to come home without a job and they sleep under cars. A grown man can't get a job, how can a little kid? Oh, Miz Wheeler, it takes a heap of hope to keep me goin', I tell you."

Ruth wanted to leave. She wanted to stand up and tell Annie Scoates good-bye and never come back. She wanted to know that when she touched the doorknob and walked outside, it would be the last time she would see Annie's blackened mouth, her half-closed eye and wrinkled face, and smell the stench of her poverty. She wanted to hear no more about gravy in baby bottles and boys stealing milk from porches. She wanted nothing to do with people who couldn't help themselves. But she did not stand up and she didn't leave, and she knew that in spite of her feelings about the baby, she was changing somehow. It was as though the sight and the stench of Annie's poverty had touched her in a way that made her more human. She didn't know quite how.

She heard her mother say that it was time to go.

"Lord, Miz Wheeler, may He bless you, comin' out all this way in the winter and spendin' train fare. All for my Benjamin."

"It's not just for Benjamin, Annie. It's for me too. There's something about talking with you that makes me feel better."

"When you can't do nothin' else, there's always talkin'. When Benjamin gets old enough, I'll tell him all about Charles, you know I will."

"Good-bye, Annie. Take care of yourself."

"Good-bye. Good-bye, Ruthie."

"Good-bye, Annie. I . . . hope the twins are better soon."

"Thank the Good Lord it's no worse than chicken pox," said Annie.

She stood in the doorway with her arms folded as they walked across the crusty snow in the yard. Mother did not look around again, and Ruth knew it was because she was leaving a little piece of Charles behind.

It was a silent ride home, and Ruth was glad that her mother did not feel like talking to her. The disgust she had felt for Annie before was tempered with despair, as though she were glimpsing the slow turn of events that makes life become something it never should have been at all.

But do things have to be this way, she wondered. Do people have to smell and look ugly and just sit around waiting for things to get worse? What would she do if she were Annie Scoates, with no education and four children? She didn't know. Mending, maybe? Buy a sewing machine? With what? Perhaps life was impossible to control after all, but then, why try? And giving up was not in her nature.

Even after they got off the IC and walked the four blocks to the house, Ruth and her mother didn't speak, each lost in her own thoughts. Once inside the front door, however, Ruth heard the voice of a stranger coming from the living room. Dawn hurried out to them.

"It's a boarder!" she whispered excitedly. "Daddy showed him the room and he likes it!"

"Oh, thank God!" Mother breathed. "I wonder how much he can pay."

"Grace," came Joe Wheeler's voice, "I'd like you to meet Michael Burke."

And as Ruth came into the living room with her mother, she saw a tall young man of nineteen rise up from the sofa and shake hands.

CHAPTER 6

February 15, 1933

Dear Diary:

It really seems strange having someone in Charles's room again, but I think it will work out OK. By the time Dawn and I get up in the morning, Michael's already dressed and gone, and on weekends he sleeps later than anybody.

At first I wasn't sure I'd like him. I guess it's the pockmarks on his face. Once you get to know him, though, you don't even notice them anymore. We talk about all kinds of things, Michael and

Kitty and me, even politics! Michael said that he read once about all the ruby and diamond cuff links that Franklin Roosevelt owns. He says he doesn't see how one man can have that while other people don't even have food, and that a man who would sit around in rubies couldn't know very much about running a country, but at least he deserves a chance.

Clyde called again tonight. Sometimes he acts like he really likes me a lot. I wish I knew for sure.

Ruth leaned over the pile of clothes at the bottom of the chute and began sorting them into smaller heaps, dropping all of the white things into the old washing machine, which alternately chugged and groaned from the center of the basement floor, surrounded by tubs of half-warm water.

Michael Burke was perched on a high stool in one corner, stitching together his leather belt, which had fallen apart along the crease. One leg rested easily on the floor, the other on a rung of the stool, making his knee jut out at an angle and emphasizing the length of his legs. His sandy hair fell down over one eye, and every so often he reached up and shoved it back. His face itself gave the impression of having been stretched, as though molded of rubber, for the space between his nose and his upper lip was unusually long. Below the mouth, an even larger chin came halfway down his neck.

Ichabod Crane, Ruth thought, glancing at him and smiling. In spite of all that and the pockmarks too, however, he was not ugly. Not handsome, but not ugly. She liked having him about on Saturdays. On weekdays he loaded trucks at a warehouse from seven in the morning till three, and Saturday evenings he washed dishes in a restaurant. But during the day he stayed around the house, got his clothes in order, and wrote letters home.

"Well," Michael was saying, "the obvious thing to do would be to ask him. Just come right out and ask him how much he likes you."

"That wouldn't work, Michael! That's a dumb idea! He'd make a joke of it."

"You're right," Michael said. "He couldn't really measure it in pounds or inches anyway, could he." Michael stopped to rethread the thick needle he was holding. "Does Clyde ever talk to Kitty about you? Ever tell her anything?"

"Only kidding, that's all. That's all he ever does. He's sort of conceited in a way. I think he gets some kind of satisfaction out of keeping me guessing."

Michael shrugged. "Could be. Some guys are like that, I guess. Bring him around some time when I'm here, and maybe I could ask him."

Ruth picked up the laundry stick and poked at the white shirts and sheets being tossed temperamentally about in the machine. "He doesn't come over very much. Mostly he just calls, or we meet somewhere—walk around, buy ice cream—things like that."

"Ask him to come over."

"How? What reason would I give?"

Michael gave an exasperated bleat. "Do you have to have a reason? Isn't it enough that you want to see him?"

"I couldn't tell him *that!* I mean, it would have to be a party or something."

"So give a party. Ask a bunch of people."

"But what would we do?"

"Dance . . . sing . . . what do you ever do at a party? I'll entertain."

Ruth broke into a laugh. "What would you do, Michael? Stand on your head?"

The tall boy grinned. "Listen, sister, you've never heard anything till you've heard Michael Burke play the harmonica. And magic? Why, I could put a penny in Clyde's ear and make it come out your nostril. I could turn a red pencil into a blue one and push a drinking glass right through the dining room table."

Ruth smiled and shook her head. "It's a great idea, but it wouldn't work. We can't afford it. Wouldn't be anything to feed them."

"That bad, huh?"

"That bad. Besides, you'd be so busy entertaining you'd forget to ask Clyde about me, and then it would be all that work for nothing."

"Ruth?" Mother's voice sounded at the top of

the stairs. "Don't you have the first load done yet? Mr. Nesbitt needs a shirt for Sunday service, and I've got to hang it out on the line while there's still full sun."

"I'm rinsing now, Mother," Ruth said, hurriedly grabbing a handful of white things from the soapy water and feeding them one at a time through the wringer into the first rinse.

"That's the difference between Chicago and Mendota," Michael said.

"What is?"

"Back in Mendota, everybody washes clothes on Monday. You go down the street at noon on a Monday, and there isn't a house hardly that doesn't have clothes out on the line. Here in Chicago they do it whenever they want." He chuckled. "Mom'll never believe me when I tell her that my landlady's daughter washes clothes on Saturday. She'll say that means you're sorting and folding on the Lord's Day, and boy, in Mendota you better believe in Sunday."

Ruth laughed. "Is that what you tell your mother when you write? All about us?"

"Sure. Why not? She's afraid I'm sleeping in an alley somewhere. Scared I'm not eating. So I tell her what I had for breakfast, what I had for lunch, what I had for supper, and that takes up half a page. You know—real zingy letters like that." Michael lifted up the belt and gnawed at the thread till he'd cut it in half. "I don't tell her everything, though. I sure don't tell her everything."

Ruth swung the wringer around to the second rinse tub and fed the clothes through again. "What don't you tell her?"

"About the jungles, that's what."

"The jungles?"

Michael smiled slightly. "It's just a word guys use to describe places where men camp, waiting for work. Christ! Men living like dogs, I swear it. One old fellow went to sleep one night on some newspapers and covered himself with a road map. Thought he was lucky to have them for covers. In the morning he was dead. Old as my grandfather. No old man ought to be sleeping out in a field like that."

Michael put the belt aside and began working on one of his shoes with a loose sole. The needle wouldn't penetrate, however, so he gave up.

"It could have been worse, though. I heard of men who would steal or kill for fifty cents. But I never saw any like that. Only jungles I stayed in, hitchhiking over from Mendota, everybody was friendly. Everybody shared what he had. One fellow, I remember, all he had was a potato. Cut it in half and gave me a piece. Just little things like that.

"First night I got to Chicago, I stayed in a jungle over by a factory. One guy had a big pot and everybody who could put a little something in it—cabbage, onions, beans. . . . A butcher gave us a soup bone, and I still remember that marvelous smell. It's not what you're eating that determines how it tastes—it all depends how hungry you are. A man gets pretty ingenious, though, when his stomach's talking to him all the time. Guys I know used to go buy a cup of coffee for a nickel, then ask for a refill with hot water. They'd take the catsup bottle off the counter, pour some in the hot water, and have a bowl of tomato soup. The same thing with iced tea. Save the lemon afterwards and some sugar cubes and make a glass of lemonade."

"How did you find our house?" Ruth asked, curious.

"Fellow said a guy who drove the ice truck knew of a place where I could get a room. I had to get me a place where Mom could write, or she'd worry herself to death."

Ruth swung the wringer around once more and the clothes dropped one at a time, flat and twisted, into the basket below. She picked it up and started up the stairs, then stopped. "You can't really afford our room, can you, Michael?"

Michael grinned. "Let's just say I'm not saving much to send to Mom. But I get my meals here, and that's a lot. Maybe next week I'll find a better job. Nothing to do back in Mendota—not even dishes on a Saturday night."

During February, Chicago's Mayor Cermak was

shot to death in Miami while riding in a car with Roosevelt. Joe Wheeler predicted a revolution unless the economy improved. Across the ocean, flames gutted the German *Reichstag*, and news commentators talked darkly of Mussolini's Blackshirts and trouble in Latin America. Ruth's father took comfort of a sort in the fact that the whole world was in turmoil and listened to a number of newscasts each evening, absorbed in what he said would one day be history.

Ruth's interests were more immediate, however. She was concerned with the fact that Chicago's teachers had been forced to accept scrip instead of money, to be redeemed after the Depression, even though the banks would not accept it.

Every day when she walked into her English class, she expected to find that Miss Harley had left, and that a new hard-eyed teacher with no soul for words or language had taken her place. But the small, slim woman was always there, and the spark that Ruth loved never seemed to go out, always waiting under the surface to be set off by a poem or a reading.

But was it really worth it, Ruth wanted to know. It seemed now that if she, herself, ever got through college, it would be by an enormous amount of hard work and sacrifice and faith and luck. And when, or if, she did get to teach, what would be the reward? Payless paydays. Worthless paper called scrip.

She longed to talk to Miss Harley about it. She wanted an answer, a secret sign, a look, even, to tell her whether to try for it or not. And so one morning she rose early and got to school soon after the janitor arrived, seeking out Miss Harley in the long silent corridors as though she were searching for the Oracle of Delphi.

Ruth was surprised when she actually found her, seated in the English office, still bundled in her coat, and drinking coffee.

"Ruth! What on earth are you doing in school at this hour?"

"I . . . I didn't think you'd be here this early either," Ruth said, sitting down as the teacher motioned to a chair beside her.

"Well, sometimes I have to hitchhike to work when the money runs low, and this morning was one of those days. I was lucky, though—someone brought me right to the door, so I'm early."

"I've been hearing about how the teachers aren't being paid," Ruth said. "I think it's just awful."

Miss Harley took another sip of coffee. "Of course it's awful. But whenever a city has to cut back somewhere, teachers are the first ones asked to sacrifice. It's always been that way it seems."

"But why?"

Little laugh lines crinkled up around Miss Harley's eyes, but this time they looked like tired lines, discouraged lines, and Ruth did not like them.

"Because we are supposed to be noble and unselfish, my dear. We are supposed to be so in love with our profession that material things don't matter—so imbued with the thought of service and self-sacrifice that food and clothes are unimportant." She gave a little laugh, and Ruth did not like the sound of it, either. "It's a good thing I live with my sister and that she has a job that pays money or I couldn't continue teaching. I couldn't afford to."

Ruth did not want to hear any more. This was not what she had expected at all. She had come here looking for hope and inspiration and found bitterness instead. She picked up her books, and a feeling of numbness spread over her as she stood up.

"I guess . . . if you could do it all over again . . . you'd be something else," she murmured, not knowing what else to say.

"Oh, no!" Miss Harley looked up at her, and the laugh lines had disappeared. Her blue eyes were serious again in the oval face that Ruth had come to love. "Oh, no! I didn't say that. I would go through it all again, Ruth, and become a teacher even if I'd known I'd have to hitchhike to work. I wouldn't let anything in the world stop me, not even this."

Relief and gratefulness and hope surged through Ruth again, like sunshine through a dark window. She wanted to hug her teacher, but she knew she couldn't.

"I'm glad, Miss Harley," she said quickly. And

suddenly she was out in the hall, walking rapidly toward her first class. She wanted to hear only that and nothing more. If, in spite of all this, Miss Harley would choose teaching above everything else, then it was indeed something very, very special, worth working for no matter what. The Oracle had spoken, and Ruth had heard.

There was to be a Spring Ball at the school, and posters were already up. It was an annual event, and everyone looked forward to it.

"You like to dance?" Clyde asked Ruth one morning, stopping by her locker, and when she nodded, he said, "Let's go, then."

"He *asked* me, Kitty," Ruth said excitedly after school as the girls wrapped their long wool scarves around their necks and, holding their breath, stepped out into the freezing February air. "Honestly, he's so *casual* about everything—like he automatically assumed I'd go with him."

"He must like you a lot," Kitty observed.

There was a wistfulness in Kitty's voice that made Ruth pause. It didn't seem right, somehow —talking to Kitty so much about Clyde when there were no boys in her own life. It was unfair that a few extra inches of girl should keep boys from asking her out, when every extra inch was a part of Kitty herself, one of the sweetest girls ever.

They slid over the wet, dirty snow and said

good-bye at the corner without chatting by the street sign as they often did. The cold was too penetrating and seemed to cut them in half.

By the time she reached home, Ruth's very lungs seemed frozen by the wind. She did not notice the telephone company truck at the curb till she collided with a repairman at the front door.

"Sorry, miss," he said, holding the door open for her, and Ruth saw the telephone in his hand. She stared as he strode down the steps and into the truck. Then she turned and raced past the empty stand in the hallway and on into the kitchen.

"Mother?" she called. "Is something wrong with the phone?" Finding the downstairs empty, she clattered up to the bedrooms above. Mrs. Wheeler was stuffing goose feathers back in the newly washed pillow tickings. Her lips were firmly set, as though prepared for an argument, and as soon as Ruth saw her, she knew.

"Mother, you're not giving up the telephone?"

"We had to, Ruthie, and I know how you feel. Your father and I talked about it last night, and we knew you'd be upset. But we're giving up everything we can. We have to."

Ruth stared. Her eyes felt small and hard. For a moment she felt she couldn't even focus, even blink.

"What if Clyde tries to call me?" she asked, and her voice sounded strangely distant.

"An operator will tell him that the number's been

disconnected, that's all. You can explain it to him at school tomorrow. We're not the only family without a telephone, you know." Mother reached out and gently unwrapped the scarf from around Ruth's neck. "Honey, if Clyde's the sort of boy you think he is, and he's really interested in you, he'll ride his bike over here and talk to you. He won't let a few blocks stand in his way."

Without answering, Ruth went downstairs to the kitchen. There was nothing to eat between meals now except apples. The whole country, it seemed, ran on apples. She picked one up and sat down by the bay window in the living room, gazing dully at the bare trees separating the Wheeler's house from Mrs. Hamilton's.

Why, she wondered, did she have to live in this age, at this particular time? It was undoubtedly the worst of all possible times, unless you counted the Black Plague or the Inquisition. Just when she was growing up, just when boys were becoming interested in her—the Depression settled down over them all. Girls were divided between those like Connie Ebert who had telephones and pretty clothes and money to give parties and girls who did not—girls like Ruth who wore skirts made from their fathers' old trousers. It wasn't fair. Ruth had only one chance to be young, and this, unfortunately, was it.

Tears welled up in her eyes and she swallowed

hard, then bit angrily into the apple. By the time Dawn was fifteen, it might be all over. Dawn would have all the things Ruth hadn't. She would be popular and happy while Ruth slowly fossilized into a bitter old woman, not at all the kind of teacher she had hoped to be.

"No, I don't know what happened to your paper dolls," she snapped at Dawn. "If you can't keep track of your things, don't expect me to."

Dawn leaned against the doorway and looked at Ruth, upset and puzzled, but Ruth was too hurt herself to care.

"Dumb old, crabby old, mean old Ruth," Dawn chanted, scratching at the paint with her fingernail, sending shivers up Ruth's back.

"Cut that out! Just get out of here, will you?"

Dawn stopped scratching, but stayed where she was. "Don't have to," she snipped, tossing back one braid that had come undone and flopped about her shoulders. One pocket on her smock was ripped, and both long tan stockings sagged pitifully at the knees.

"Good heavens, Dawn, you're a mess." Ruth continued sharply, "You always look like the ragman's daughter. In fact, you look like one of Annie Scoates's kids. If you don't start caring how you look, you won't have any friends at all when you get to high school. Boys won't even come *near* you! Look. You've eaten a cracker, and you still have crumbs all over your face. A regular pig. . . ."

Dawn waited to hear no more, but bolted suddenly from the room and fled upstairs, crying.

Ruth felt sick inside. She wanted to go upstairs and tell Dawn she didn't really mean it. She wanted to say something funny to make her laugh. But the hate paralyzed her—the hate for the way things were going. So she sat woodenly in the chair, feeling the cold that seeped in around the window. Where were all her brave words now about fighting back, about not letting poverty get the best of her? Someone had just taken the telephone, and there wasn't a thing she could do about it.

Clyde said nothing at school the next day about the phone, and Ruth couldn't think of a good way to bring it up. It would sound as though she had been expecting him to call. So she said nothing. Only Kitty commented.

"Too bad it wasn't our phone," she said dryly. "Boys never call me anyway."

As the days wore on, however, the telephone became one of the lesser problems. For the first time that Ruth could remember, she experienced hunger —not a wild, aching prelude to starvation, but a feeling after each meal that she wanted more, and there wasn't any. Anything extra went to Father and Michael Burke. Potatoes became the staple food, and sometimes an entire meal consisted of cabbage or boiled potatoes and two kinds of beans flavored with a soup bone. Michael found a place that sold day-old bread for a nickel and brought some home. Food was always on their minds.

One night Ruth dreamed that she had to go somewhere on the trolley and something had happened to her clothes, she wasn't sure what. So she put on the only dress she could find, with spots on the skirt, and ran all the way to Cottage Grove only to have the driver tell her that she smelled and would have to sit by an open window. And then the other passengers began moving away from her, and she was so embarrassed that she tried to get off, but the trolley was moving again. She started to cry and immediately woke up, her legs jerking, a soft moaning sound in her throat.

She stumbled out of bed, moaning still, and stood in the middle of the floor, her heart pounding, unsure what had happened. Then she groped toward the chair in the corner and picked up the dress she had worn the day before, holding it to her face. It smelled!

Crying again, Ruth made her way out into the hall in the darkness, clutching the dress, and downstairs to the kitchen. She turned on the light in the basement and continued her trek to the washtub. Eyes half-closed against the light, tears on her cheeks, she turned on the water and plunged the dress in.

"I won't smell!" she wept, jerking the garment up and down. "I won't smell!"

"Ruth? What on earth?"

Mrs. Wheeler peered down from the top of the stairs, leaning over to see, and then hurriedly came on down, clutching her robe about her. "Honey, what in the world is the matter?"

"My dress smells, Mother!" Ruth wept. "And they all were. . . ." She stopped, realizing the dream part of it, but agitated still.

"Well, I imagine it does, sweetheart. You cleaned house in it yesterday. Is that so terrible? Nothing we can do about sweat." Gently she took the dress from Ruth and wrung it out. "Ruth, I think you were having a bad dream. You're still a little groggy. I'll wash your dress this week with the other clothes. Go on back to bed."

Ruth walked slowly upstairs and on up to her room. Her heart had stopped racing, and her mind was in focus again. It had only been a dream. There was no trolley and no people, and there were clean clothes in her closet. But the feelings had been real. For a few brief moments she had been Annie Scoates, and it was some time before she could fall asleep again.

On the first of March, Mr. Wheeler sold the car and made a mortgage payment with the money. Mother found two more customers for laundry and ironing. Even Dawn helped. She went out daily to scrounge about for empty bottles that she could take back to the store for the deposit, with old stockings on her hands in place of mittens, which had long since worn out. Ruth took over most of the housekeeping herself so that Mother could keep up with the wash. Several times a week she cooked the potatoes and beans for supper, and occasionally a floating island for dessert when they could afford the eggs. She stoically accepted the rabbit meat, which they ate when Father went on hunting trips down near the Kankakee River, even though she recoiled from those limp gray animals with glassy eyes and buckshot in their flanks.

When there was no money at all for groceries, they sold something—the company bedspread, a lamp, a pair of figurines. Or they took their most precious possessions to the pawnshop, adding a new fear to the worry about losing the house. The day Mrs. Wheeler pawned her wedding ring and cried, Joe Wheeler himself went down and bought it back with the money he had tucked away for emergencies. Now they had nothing at all to fall back on, and when Dawn came home from school saying that the principal had asked them all to bring canned goods for the poor, Mrs. Wheeler laughed bitterly. "Where will you find anybody poorer than we are?" she said, and the fear grew stronger in the pit of Ruth's stomach.

As she dusted Michael's room one evening, her

eye fell on an unfinished letter he'd been writing to his mother. For a moment she fought with herself about peeking, but finally gave in and read the last few lines:

> . . . things are going fine, and I don't want you worrying about me. Any week now, a career job will be coming through, and then you'll really see things happen . . .

The Depression made liars out of everyone, Ruth thought. Each was holding the others up with songs and jokes and stories about how prosperity was just around the corner. Nobody believed it, but no one said so. Like a string of dominoes, none could afford to let the others down.

I, Franklin Delano Roosevelt, do solemnly swear, that I will faithfully execute the office of the President of the United States, and will, to the best of my ability, preserve, protect, and defend the Constitution of the United States, so help me God.

This is a day of national confrontation, and I am certain that on this day my fellow Americans expect that on my induction into the Presidency I will address them with a candor and a decision which the present situation of our people impells.

This is preeminently the time to speak the truth, the whole truth, frankly and boldly. Nor need we shrink from honestly facing con-

ditions in our country today. This great na-
tion will endure as it has endured, will revive
and will prosper. So, first of all, let me assert
my firm belief that the only thing we have to
fear is fear itself. . . .

Ruth sat across the room from Michael Burke,
listening to the Inaugural address. Joe Wheeler
crouched on the edge of his chair, arms on his knees,
hands tense, as though Roosevelt were speaking per-
sonally to him.

The old Philco was acting up, and static drowned
out some of the words, so that when it was over, Joe
turned the radio off. "Talks like a Harvard professor," he said, "but you gotta admit that man's got
ideas. He's going to make things move. You hear
what he said about the only thing to fear is fear itself?"

But Mrs. Wheeler, sitting on the arm of his chair
with an old coat about her shoulders, stared vacantly at the opposite wall. "How do you not be
afraid, Joe? How do you do it? Going through a
depression is like walking through the dark—you
don't even know what's a step ahead of you. It
wouldn't matter what was there so much if you
could only see to get around it. It's the not knowing
that's so awful."

"*Somebody's* got to try something," Michael
commented, his long legs stretched out across the
threadbare rug. "Sure, they all talk good at

the Inauguration, and it's what comes after that counts. But I don't think he'd talk about bold new action and all that if he didn't plan to do something that hadn't been tried before."

There were soft hesitant footsteps on the stairs.

"Is that Dawn?" Mother wondered. "She fell asleep on her bed so I didn't wake her up. I wonder if she's all right."

Ruth turned toward the hall. "Are you okay, Dawn?"

Dawn came down on the bottom step. "Mother," she called weakly.

"Dawn, what's wrong?" Ruth asked, starting toward her. "Mother, she looks awful!"

Mrs. Wheeler sprang up and rushed out into the hallway. The same instant, Dawn collapsed and sank to her feet in a crumpled heap of corduroy playsuit and stocking feet.

"Oh, Lord!" Mrs. Wheeler cried, lifting up Dawn's face with her hands. "She's burning up! Joe!"

Michael Burke stood uncomfortably in the doorway, not knowing what to do, as Father knelt down beside Dawn and began rubbing her arms vigorously. "Make some ice water, Ruth, and bring a towel," he said.

"I'll chip the ice," Michael said quickly, and Ruth hurried upstairs for the towel.

Dawn was placed on her bed, but no sooner had she come to than she had a convulsion. Her eyes rolled back, her teeth clenched, and she began twitching uncontrollably.

"Joe!" Mother cried out again, terrified.

"You want me to go next door and call a doctor, Mrs. Wheeler?" Michael offered from the hall, where he waited.

"Oh, I . . . I don't know. . . . What shall we do, Joe? We haven't got the money. . . ."

"Call the doctor," Father said tersely. "Mrs. Hamilton has the number."

As Michael bounded downstairs, Ruth sat in the small rocker in one corner of Dawn's room, staring at her sister, terror rising up in her. *We can't even afford to get sick*, she thought desperately. *Only the rich can afford the luxury of being sick.* And suddenly she felt furious at Franklin Delano Roosevelt and his ruby cuff links and his big words about fearing fear itself. What did he know about living in a cold house and eating potatoes, about putting cardboard inside your shoes when the soles began wearing out?

Dawn was whimpering. She said that her throat hurt, and then she began shaking again.

There were hurried footsteps on the stairs, and Mrs. Hamilton came to the doorway, a towel around her wet hair, smelling of vinegar rinse. But she did not come in.

"Grace," she said, peering over her glasses, "I'll bet it's scarlet fever. Does your head hurt, Dawn? Ache all over?"

Dawn nodded miserably.

Mother stood with one hand on her throat, a look of complete helplessness on her face. Ruth turned away. Not scarlet fever! Hadn't a cousin died of it once?

"The doctor said he'd come by shortly," Michael said.

"Then I'd better go home, or he'll quarantine me too," Mrs. Hamilton said. "I'll check with you later, Grace. Keep her fever down if you can."

Quarantine. Ruth moved out into the hall and leaned against the doorframe. Her legs felt weak and trembly, so she made her way to the stairs and sat down, her head in her lap.

Things were closing in on her now, faster than she had imagined. It wasn't enough that she had had to start high school looking like an immigrant. It wasn't enough that her family could not afford parties for her friends. It wasn't even enough that the telephone was gone and boys couldn't call her or that she had to worry all the time about college. Now the quarantine sign would go up on the house, no one would be allowed to leave or enter, and when the three weeks were up, the Spring Ball would be over.

Angry, bitter tears seeped out of her eyes and onto her lap. She hated herself for thinking such selfish thoughts when Dawn's life was at stake. Would she never grow up?

Michael had gone downstairs with Mrs. Hamilton, and Ruth could hear her parents' worried voices from Dawn's room. A quarantine sign meant that Father would not be able to go to work, and neither would Michael. Sometimes, if the father had not been in contact with the child, he was allowed to live somewhere else for three weeks and keep his job. Should they lie to the health inspector? Should they tell him that Father and Michael had not touched Dawn, been in the same room, even? And where would they go till the quarantine was over?

The doctor came, sternly carrying his black bag up to the second floor. Ruth waited on the stairs, her head resting against the wall, eyes closed. There were the pauses in conversation, the sound of quiet footsteps about Dawn's room, questions, murmurs, and then suddenly Mother's voice saying, "Oh, what a relief! What a relief!"

Ruth opened her eyes, listened, and then hurried to the doorway.

"It's not scarlet fever, Ruth," Mother told her, her eyes glistening. "Just a bad cold. Oh, I'm so relieved."

The doctor smiled wryly. "Don't think it makes much difference to you, Dawn, does it? You still feel bad." He painted her throat with argyrol and left some camphor.

"Doc, I just don't know when I can pay you," Joe Wheeler said as they stepped out into the hall.

The doctor pulled on his gloves and said nothing.

"Lost my job, and can hardly keep food on the table. I just don't know...."

The doctor patted him on the shoulder, unsmiling. "Well, do the best you can, Joe," he said. "In a few months, maybe...."

As Mother straightened up the medicine bottles on Dawn's dresser, the thermometer rolled off onto the floor and broke. Mrs. Wheeler sat down in Dawn's rocker and cried like a small child.

Just before dinner, Kitty came over, and after talking about the Inauguration and Dawn, sat on the davenport, strangely subdued and quiet.

"Ruth, do you . . . do you still have the bracelet I gave you once for your birthday?" she asked finally.

"Of course I have it! I'd never give it up. Why?"

Kitty closed her eyes a moment and took a deep breath. "I've got to ask for it back. It was an heirloom, and we need the money. Mother's taking it to the pawnship."

Instantly Ruth felt what Kitty was going through, and she was flooded with sympathy, glad that she cared, glad that she was able to think about somebody else.

"Listen, Kitty, don't worry! It's okay. I enjoyed it for a long time. I wore it everywhere. It's only right that you should have it back. I mean, an *heirloom* and everything. I'll run right up and get it."

Ruth went upstairs to her jewelry box. When she returned, Michael was telling Kitty about the crown jewels of Russia, and how the earrings were so heavy that they pulled the earlobes half down to the shoulders. Kitty was smiling.

Bless him, Ruth said to herself as she put the bracelet in Kitty's lap. There was something about having Michael around that made the house more a home. No matter how many plagues the Depression dropped in their laps, somehow Michael made them bearable.

Ruth wished that once—just once—Clyde would treat her special. She wished that instead of casually stopping by her locker, he had come to the house and formally asked her to the dance. She wished that he would ask her what flowers she preferred, and where she would like to go afterwards.

Instead, he treated her no better or worse than he treated the other girls at school, and it was only when they met at the drugstore on Saturday night or strolled around the park and the high school on Sundays that she got his complete attention. Still, it was she who was his choice for the dance, and she was determined to walk into that gym looking great. With Kitty's help, of course.

They looked over the clothes in Vera's closet one afternoon after school.

"This one!" Kitty exclaimed, pulling out a thin lavender dress with a rose of the same material at the bosom. "Ruth, it would be perfect on you!"

"You don't think it would be too cold?"

"If it is, you could wear Vera's white shawl."

"Kitty, I can't just walk in here and take over Vera's closet! How do you know she'll let me?"

"Because she'd let me if I was going, and you're practically my sister."

Ruth held the dress against her and looked in the mirror. The neckline was low, and she blushed. Maybe if they moved the rose up a little higher. . . . She swished from side to side and watched the ripples of lavender fall about her thighs. Kitty was right. It was perfect.

"Tell him you want white flowers," Kitty said, walking with her through the grocery to the sidewalk again, ducking her head under the cheese and salami that hung just inside the door. "They'll go with anything. If you tell him the dress is lavender, he might feel he had to get an orchid, and he could never afford one."

"That's a good idea, Kitty," Ruth said. "I'll remember."

There was something about the way Kitty stood there in the doorway of the grocery, hugging herself with her arms, that reminded Ruth of Michael when he came down to breakfast on Saturday mornings, leaning against the kitchen doorway only half awake. And as Ruth turned back down the sidewalk toward home, she wondered suddenly if there was any reason on earth why Michael couldn't take Kitty to the dance. Why hadn't

she thought of that before? Kitty liked Michael—
as a friend, at least—and that was enough.

Mrs. Wheeler was upstairs bathing Dawn when
Ruth got home. Michael, who got home quite early
from his job, was already on a stepladder in the dining room, cleaning the walls with a big green glob
of wallpaper cleaner. As he rubbed it over a panel
of lily print, the grayness vanished and the cream-
colored lilies brightened. Slowly he worked his way
along, bits of cleaner falling to the floor.

"Hi," he said, scarcely even looking down.
"What's new?"

"Lots." Ruth took off her coat, realized the room
was cold, and put it back over her shoulders.
"How's Dawn?"

"We think she's got the flu now. Poor kid isn't
ever going to get well." He tossed Ruth a bunch of
cleaner. "Make yourself useful."

Ruth took off her coat and came over to the
ladder, stretching up to the place where Michael
had left off and rubbing down the wall from there.

"I always liked the smell of wallpaper cleaner,"
Michael was saying. "Whenever Mom opened a
can, I'd want to smell it. Weird, huh?"

"I always liked gasoline, myself," Ruth told him.
"And citronella."

"Yeah, and camphor. Camphor's great!"

Ruth slowly stopped working. "Michael, would
you like to make somebody really, really happy?"

"Depends. Hey, don't stop. We've got two whole walls to do yet. What do you want me to do. Your math?"

"Ask Kitty to a dance at school."

The clump of cleaner fell out of Michael's hand, but he caught it with the other.

"How can I ask Kitty? I don't go to the school. I'm not even supposed to know there's a dance."

"Well, I'll have her ask you, then, and promise you'll say yes. It's the big Spring Ball and everybody's going. Clyde's taking me, and nobody's asked Kitty because she's so tall."

"Look, Ruth. I like Kitty and all that, but I'm broke. I'm perpetually broke! I've been broke ever since I was born!"

The marvelous bubble of an idea burst. Ruth hadn't even given it a thought. The whole world and everything in it ran on money. Everything she wanted to do had a price. She leaned heavily against the wall, kneading the wad of cleaner in her hand.

But it wasn't as hopeless as she'd thought. It occurred to her suddenly that Kitty was on the decorating committee and would get a ticket free. If both she and Kitty agreed to go without flowers, it wouldn't be so bad as if just one girl alone was without them. And as for afterwards, a place to go . . . well, they could think of something. She sat down on a chair and detailed it for Michael.

"Sure. Why not?" he said from the top of the ladder, and Ruth reached up and hugged his legs in jubilation. "One thing, though. Better not tell Kitty it was your idea. Tell her I said I wouldn't mind taking her to the dance myself if she'd just ask me. I mean, we tall people have our pride."

Ruth wanted to be at school early the next day to tell Kitty, but Mother asked her to change Dawn's sheets before she went. By the time she reached the north door of the building, Kitty had already gone in. When she turned the corner to her locker, however, she came face to face with Clyde.

"Clyde!" she said, and even to herself her voice sounded beautiful. She was at her best, she decided, when she was taken by surprise—when there wasn't time to ruin the spontaneity.

"How you doing?" Clyde said. "Listen, I need to talk to you. . . ."

There was no time, however. The second bell drowned out his voice and left their ears clanging even after it had stopped.

"I'll be here after school," Ruth suggested.

"No, I've got to help my uncle move some lumber. How about tomorrow morning—eight-fifteen?"

"Sure."

He squeezed her elbow. "See you then."

At ten, Ruth and Kitty met in the library.

"Vera said you could wear the dress," Kitty told her, "but not the white shawl. We couldn't afford to have it dry cleaned."

Ruth could hardly contain her excitement. She

struggled to keep her voice calm. "What do you suppose *you'll* wear, Kitty?"

Kitty squinted down at her. "What'll I wear? My pajamas, probably, since I'll be going to bed."

Ruth grabbed her arm, unable to hold back any longer. "No you won't, Kitty. Somebody wants you to ask him. You'll never guess who."

"Wants *me* to ask *him!*"

A dark green dress suddenly came between them, and a stern voice said, "If you ladies *must* talk, will you continue your conversation in the hall, please?"

Embarrassed, Ruth gathered up her books under the librarian's glare and went outside, followed by Kitty.

"Who?" Kitty choked, pouncing on her again.

"Michael."

"Michael Burke? Ruth, did he really? What did he say? Tell me exactly what he said."

Ruth related a nonexistent, but convincing conversation in which Michael longed to go to the dance, and wondered if Kitty liked him enough to ask him. "Oh, Kitty, we'll have a wonderful time! Clyde and Michael will get along fine! I know it!"

Kitty listened, her cheeks pink, numb with delight. "How old is he, Ruth?"

"Nineteen. Oh, Kitty, you'll be the envy of the whole school. I mean, you're practically going with a *man!*"

"What if Clyde has other plans, Ruth? What if

he's arranged for you to double with someone else?"

The thought had never occurred to Ruth, but it was too late to back out now. "Then you and Michael will go alone. But you've got to ask him, Kitty. Come home with me after school. I mean, he's got to have time to make plans."

Michael had just arrived home from work and was eating a cold cooked potato when Ruth walked into the kitchen. She sent him out on the porch to talk to Kitty, potato in hand, and watched discreetly from the window.

It was embarrassing watching—like looking at the old silent movies, understanding without hearing. Michael perched himself on the porch railing, one hand holding onto the latticework along the side, and Kitty leaned against the wall, her long legs entwined at the ankles, a picture of self-consciousness. But gradually Michael's easy banter won her over, the ankles untwined, and she laughed and seemed more herself. And after Kitty went home and Michael went up to his room whistling, Ruth felt she had done something tremendously wonderful and good.

Ruth arrived at school at a quarter past eight the following morning, and Clyde was already there, leaning against her locker chewing a stick of gum. When he saw Ruth, he took the gum out and wrapped it in paper.

"Hi," Ruth said, smiling and wondering if he'd

noticed the new way she'd parted her hair. It looked, she felt, particularly soft and shiny.

Clyde, however, didn't really look at her at all. As she opened her locker and hung up her coat, he kept his eyes turned to the corridor instead, as if watching the distant clock.

"Listen, Ruth, you weren't really counting on that dance, were you? I mean, you didn't really take me seriously. . . ."

Ruth turned slowly around and looked at him. She couldn't believe it.

"I mean, it just occurred to me that maybe you were making plans for the dance or something, and I'm always shooting off my big mouth."

She tried hard to make her voice sound normal. "I thought you asked me to go."

He gave a little laugh and shifted his weight to the other foot, thrusting his hands deeper down in his pockets. "Gees, I never thought it sounded all that definite. I mean, it was just an idea."

He was looking at her now. He seemed acutely embarrassed, and suddenly Ruth felt sorry for him. He couldn't afford it. That must be the reason. She would show him that she understood, that it didn't matter. . . . But he was talking again.

"Listen, Ruth, it's sort of complicated, but I've got to take someone else. I mean, I'd *rather* take you, but something came up, and I've got to help someone out. Gees, if I'd thought you were really counting on it, though, I'd never . . . I mean, if I'd thought you took me seriously. . . ."

Ruth picked up her books and shut the locker. She was too angry to speak, but she was *glad* she was angry. It was better to be angry than to be hurt, better to fight than be walked on, better that Clyde should see fire in her eyes than tears.

"Aw, Ruth, don't get mad. I mean, it's really complicated. It's a mess. But I promised. . . ."

She began walking down the hall, faster and faster, Clyde running to keep up, until suddenly he stopped abruptly, and there was only the sound of her own footsteps in the corridor. She reached her empty classroom and sank down in a chair near the back.

Kitty was working in the cafeteria two days a week, and so Ruth was able to avoid eating with her this time. She passed her once in the hall, smiled bravely, and said she'd see her tomorrow, and left as soon as school was out. She wanted to see no one, talk to no one. And because she kept it locked inside her, she found no sympathy when she got home.

There was a sack of oranges on the kitchen table, and Ruth knew they were for Dawn and didn't touch them. No matter how poor the family might be, there were always oranges when someone was sick. At that moment Mrs. Wheeler came down from upstairs, and she moved with a decisiveness that always characterized her when she wanted no arguments.

"Dawn any better?" Ruth asked numbly.

"Her temperature's down some, but she's still so weak she can hardly get to the bathroom." Mrs. Wheeler pressed her lips together, avoiding her daughter's eyes. "Tonight, Ruth, we lose our pride. I want you to take this kettle and go to the soup kitchen for our dinner."

What did it matter? What was one more degradation? Ruth put her coat on again without a word. Mrs. Wheeler noticed her silence and wanted to explain.

"The doctor's coming by soon, and I have to be here to talk with him. And I certainly can't ask Michael to go for us. Dawn needs all the nourishment she can get. It's the least you can do for your sister."

Still Ruth said nothing. She picked up the kettle and headed for the soup kitchen. She couldn't think. Her mind was in shock. It helped to keep moving, keep walking, avoiding the soul-searching that had to come.

The line was two blocks long, but it moved fairly quickly, and Ruth could tell by the way people talked that they were regulars. The women wore heavy coats, too big or too small for them, and passed the time discussing which days of the week the soup was the best, depending on when the restaurants sent their leftovers to make the broth.

A girl standing behind Ruth nudged her as they rounded the corner, nearing the kitchen.

"When you get up to the man," she confided, "say, 'dig down deep,' or else he'll just skim you the broth off the top and there'll be hardly any meat and potatoes at all."

Ruth pretended not to hear. Her face burned. She would die before she said that. She kept her face forward, ignoring the chatter of the girl, who was fussing now at her brother and wiping her nose on her sleeve.

Ruth thought how often she had seen these lines from the window of her father's car, never once believing she would some day be standing in one. Her family were not ordinary beggars of the Depression, she told herself. It was simply that Dawn was sick, and they needed something extra . . . but what did it matter? What did anything matter?

They neared the steam table, and the aroma of carrots and onions drifted out over the cold sidewalk. Ruth stepped forward and handed her kettle to the man with the ladle. The girl behind nudged her again, but Ruth could not open her mouth. She wanted to tell them that she didn't really belong here—that her sister was sick—but she said nothing, and watched helplessly as the man ladled out six big cupfuls from the top of the pot, sloshing it over the sides, and thrust the kettle back to her again.

"Dig down deep!" sang out the girl behind her, as

she stepped up for her turn, and gave Ruth a contemptuous look.

Trouble, Ruth had already discovered, always came in twos or threes. When something bad happened, more was sure to follow, and it did not really surprise her when she saw Connie Ebert and a friend coming down the sidewalk behind her just as she turned and headed home. They were just coming back from gymnastics class, she figured, and were probably heading for the doughnut shop. Pulling the collar of her coat up high about her neck, she felt she could escape detection. Besides, they seemed absorbed in their conversation and she was sure they had not seen her. As she moved along with the soup kettle, her face turned in toward the store windows, she heard their voices growing louder till they were almost upon her heels.

". . . Hal is picking them up first and then coming for me," Connie Ebert was saying. "Then we'll all come back to my place afterwards for the party."

Ruth swallowed, concentrating on a display in a window.

"How did you get Clyde to ask her?" the other girl was saying.

Connie gave a little laugh, like the high tinkling of a bell. "Clyde'll do anything for me. I told him I had a girl friend who was dying to meet him, and I sort of hinted that if he asked Norma, they could double with us and go in Hal's car. And Hal's got a great car."

The words grew dimmer as the girls passed Ruth and moved on.

"I wish Mitch could drive. I get so tired of walking everywhere we go. . . ."

"The last time we went out, we . . ."

Ruth stopped in a doorway and set the kettle down. She felt as though her whole body had turned to ice. For a moment she felt she couldn't catch her breath, and then she was weak all over. She wanted to pour the soup in the gutter. She wanted to tear off the shabby coat and the shoes that were worn at the heels and run and run until she was far away. Most of all, she never wanted to see Clyde again. She knew now why it was he had chosen to walk around the park with on weekends: because she was poor and would never expect anything better. He couldn't afford anyone else. But when he had the chance to ride in Hal's car and go to Connie's party, he had dropped Ruth with the barest of excuses. Ruth had been better for his ego than no girl at all. But now he didn't need her.

At home, she set the kettle mechanically on the stove in the kitchen and took off her coat, her face drawn. Mrs. Wheeler ran a spoon through the broth.

"If that's what they call soup, no wonder people are starving," she commented. "You'd think they'd put something in it." She stopped and looked at her daughter. "Why, Ruth! What's the matter?"

Ruth ate nothing. She sat in the living room and

stared out the bay window into the darkness. It was the end of so much before there was even a proper beginning.

CHAPTER 7

March 14, 1933

Dear Diary:

  *I think I knew all along that this would happen—
that something would happen. I wonder if Clyde
really liked me at all. He was probably just flattered
at the dumb way Kitty and I used to hang around
his house. Every time I think of it now I could die.
Kitty says she thinks he'd really rather take me instead of Norma Brown and is just doing it to please
Connie, but that doesn't make me feel better at all.*

  A big box of clothes came today from Aunt

Clara. There were a lot of dresses and skirts of Linda's that fit me perfectly. Mother says it's an answer to prayer. Whatever, it's the only nice thing that's happened all week. No, the second nice thing, I guess. Roosevelt gave a talk on the radio last Sunday about having faith in our banks, and the newspaper said that more people made deposits yesterday than withdrawals. Father says it's a good sign. But I don't see how it's going to do us any good. I hate this Depression almost more than Clyde Heidelberger.

The family treated Ruth with a quiet kindness that both helped and hurt. She felt alternately like a loved, protected daughter and an ugly, pitied stepchild.

Mercifully, she had seen Clyde only once in the entire week, and then from a distance. He had flushed when he saw her, and she had looked the other way, glad that she had made him uncomfortable. But it was a hollow kind of victory. She went back and forth to school each day in a kind of nothingness, and Kitty trudged numbly along beside her, unable to understand how it could have turned out this way.

Ruth didn't want to talk about it. For the first time she knew what it was like to be Kitty—to sit on the sidelines and watch a friend making plans, going places. Kitty had never complained. She had always been enthusiastic and helpful, and Ruth knew that it was her turn now to do the same. But one thought kept coming back over and over again, and each time it surfaced, she shoved it under, trampled on it, and pretended she hadn't thought it: if she had not arranged for Kitty to ask Michael to go, she could have asked him herself. She would have gone to the dance after all, and wouldn't Clyde have been surprised to see her there with a man of nineteen? But it was too late.

"Michael's pretty excited about the dance, Kitty," Ruth said with false cheerfulness. "Last night he spent a half-hour polishing his shoes. You'll make the best-looking couple there."

Kitty squirmed in anguish. "Oh, Ruth, how will I have any fun if you're not there?" she protested.

"It's not the end of the world," Ruth said. She didn't really believe it, but it helped to be angry. It helped give her spirit. Clyde Heidelberger was just another part of the Depression, the part that made boys jump at the chance for a little glamor, a little show. She wouldn't let anything get her down—not even this. Perhaps this had even happened to Miss Harley once, and somehow she had survived it.

On Friday, Ruth had just set the table for dinner when Michael came in the back door. He was smiling cockily, and slipped a white container in the icebox.

"Dessert," he said. He did a short tap dance in

front of the stove, threw his jacket up in the air and caught it again, whirled around, and danced his way into the dining room.

Ruth smiled in spite of herself. She was pleased when she realized that she genuinely wanted him to enjoy the evening—pleased that she was capable of caring for somebody else when she felt so lonely inside. Compassion. Empathy. That's what she admired in Miss Harley. Was she beginning to develop it, too?

Dinner that evening was gay. Ruth was determined not to think about the number of girls who were getting dressed that very minute for the dance. Michael was in exceptionally good spirits and kept up a steady banter with Dawn, who looked like herself again for the first time in several weeks. It would have been such a wonderful night if only Ruth were going.

"So the hermit's finally decided she's well enough to come out of her room and eat with the rest of the family, huh?" Michael said, peering at Dawn. He folded his bread over double before he took a bite. "Hair's grown a foot, you know it? That's what happens to hermits when they put themselves away. Hair and toenails get so long they can't even walk."

Dawn giggled.

"And their voices!" Michael rolled his eyes. "Oh, brother, their voices get all low and gravelly because they never talked to anybody for twenty years!"

"Mine isn't!" Dawn insisted, speaking so high that she positively squeaked. "And my toenails aren't long either. You just made that up, Michael, so I'd come downstairs."

"Why would I want you downstairs? Why, less folks there are at the table, the more food there is for me. Here I thought you were going to live up there the rest of your life, and now you're down here eating all the cornbread before I can get my hands on any."

Joe Wheeler spooned a bite of stew into his mouth, grinning. "Now you know what it'd be like to have a brother around, Dawn. Why, if Charles was here, you wouldn't have a moment's peace."

At that moment Kitty knocked on the front door and came on back to the kitchen.

"Kitty!" they all said together when she appeared in the doorway, and Ruth stared. It was a beautiful Kitty who stood there in a green dress, her hair softly waved on one side, a hint of rouge and lipstick, and a long necklace that hung down beneath her waist.

"Kitty, you're gorgeous!" Ruth told her sincerely.

"What a lovely dress, dear," Mrs. Wheeler exclaimed. "Doesn't she look lovely, Michael?"

"She looks great. I knew she would."

Suddenly Michael reached over and took Ruth's plate away. "Okay, that's enough," he said mysteriously. "Time to get dressed."

Ruth stared at him. "What?"

"You're going with us," he said.

"I am not!" Ruth declared. "You're crazy, Michael. I wouldn't go for anything in the world!"

"Oh, yes, you are going," Kitty said. "Michael and I have it all figured out. I brought over Vera's lavender dress, and I'm here to help you get ready."

"Mother!" Ruth began helplessly.

"Well, I don't know anything about this," Mrs. Wheeler said, "but if you're going to be on time, you'd better get ready. Go get in the tub, and I'll heat the curling iron."

"I'm not *going!*" Ruth bleated. "I'm not walking in there with Michael and Kitty like I'd tagged along for the evening. What would everyone say?"

"Who cares what anybody says?" Micahel asked. "There will be other singles there—boys, at least. There always were when I was in school. If anybody asks, I'll say I couldn't decide between you."

"Kitty, this is ridiculous!" Ruth said, but Michael took her arm and pulled her up from the table. "I can't go!"

"If you don't get dressed, we'll take you as you are," Michael threatened, "and that will really be something."

Ruth looked down at her spotted skirt and wrinkled blouse.

"Come on," urged Kitty and pulled Ruth toward the stairs. "You can argue with us on the way there. If you don't hurry, we'll all be late."

"This is just about the dumbest thing!" Ruth began again, but Mother had the bath water running, and Ruth gave in.

Dutifully, Ruth got in the tub and out again and sat still while her mother curled her hair and Kitty did her nails. She tried to keep her mind positively blank. She knew that if she gave it even a minute's thought, she would stay home. But she couldn't help wondering whether, if she had been Kitty, she would have been so willing to have another girl along. She wasn't sure, and it made her ashamed. Kitty was really special. Michael didn't know just how lucky he was.

The hair was curled, the nails were clean, and Ruth carefully pulled on her silk stockings, the only good pair she owned. Lifting her arms above her head, she felt Vera's lavender dress brush down over her shoulders and around her hips, swishing softly as it fell.

"What a beautiful thing!" Mrs. Wheeler breathed. "Here, Ruth, Dad polished your shoes. See, the scuff marks hardly show."

Ruth slipped them on and stepped in front of the mirror. She was beautiful. She really was.

"Oh, Kitty!" she said, whirling around suddenly. "Are you sure you don't mind?"

"I couldn't be happier."

There were more surprises. Michael met them at the bottom of the stairs with the white box in his hands. He gave it to Kitty, and Ruth realized it wasn't dessert at all. Inside were two gardenias, one for each girl.

"Michael!" Ruth scolded. "You couldn't afford these!"

"So I stole them," Michael grinned.

"You didn't!"

"I made deliveries last Saturday for Serio's, and they paid me in gardenias," he confessed.

Ruth's eyes grew moist, but she knew if she cried it would streak her powder.

"Thank you, Michael," she said simply, and put the flower on her wrist, holding it out for Dawn to smell. "It's the first one I ever had, and it's really beautiful."

"You're all a sight for sore eyes!" Mr. Wheeler said. "If I had the car, I'd drive you. Dressed like that, you should go in class."

"It's a good night for walking," Michael said. He offered both arms to the girls.

"This is positively insane," Ruth giggled as they started down the steps.

"Well, it's a good night for insanity, too," Michael added. "Full moon."

The giggling was infectious, and they laughed all the way to the school.

I wonder if this is how it feels to be drunk, Ruth thought as Michael hung their coats on the rack outside the gymnasium. *I feel giddy and silly and I just don't care what anybody says and I'm glad I feel this way because I'd never go if I didn't.*

Michael made a remark that Ruth didn't catch, but she laughed anyway, partly out of nervousness, and they moved through the glass doors to the festooned gym with its twinkling streamers and gray-blue balloons clustered like clouds on the ceiling.

A few people near the door turned and looked as they entered, but other couples whirled past them on the floor without a second glance.

Michael handed the ticket Kitty had given him to the chaperone at the door, then opened his wallet and paid for one for Ruth.

"Courtesy of your father," he whispered. Then he deftly guided them over to the refreshment table on the far side of the gym.

"Now Ruth," he said, filling a cup with punch and sitting her down on the long row of chairs along the wall, "if anyone asks, your partner has stepped out for a moment. Okay?" He filled another cup and set it down beside her as though reserving the chair. Then, his arm around Kitty, he walked out on the dance floor.

They were, Ruth decided, one of the handsomest couples there. Kitty's head reached Michael's eyebrows, and their long limbs and bodies moved well together. Unless one looked closely, he would not notice that Michael's suit coat and trousers did not match. His tie was one of Joe Wheeler's, and his brown shoes had been polished black for the occasion. In the dimness of the vast gymnasium, however, few could tell, and Ruth noticed that he stayed away from the well-lit circle in the middle of the floor where the more showy couples danced.

They had only been on the floor a minute when the music was over. Michael stood where they'd stopped, holding Kitty's hand in his, and waited for the next number. Everything he did seemed so sophisticated, so suave, as though he had been around a very long time. The next song was slower, and his arm slid around Kitty's waist again, drawing her to him, and they began to dance, their faces close.

Ruth had never seen Kitty in anyone's arms before, and she was surprised how natural Kitty looked in Michael's. Somehow Ruth had expected her to look self-conscious and awkward. Instead, she seemed to belong there, as if all the months of being alone had prepared her well for the moment when a boy would embrace her.

The music ended, and it was Kitty's turn to sit out a number. Ruth found herself being whirled out on the floor in Michael's strong arms, moving to his sure step.

"I'll say one thing for Mendota," she joked, "they sure taught you to dance."

"My natural talent," he teased.

Ruth had not realized before just how tall Michael really was. She scarcely reached his shoulder. She was conscious of the strength of his hand behind her back, the forcefulness of his lead, the fragrance of his hair tonic, the muscles in his arms. . . .

A clarinet player rose in the band for a few solo phrases, and Ruth closed her eyes for a moment, lost in the music.

When she opened them again, she saw Clyde and his date dancing toward them not five yards away. Clyde was talking, looking down at Norma as he danced nearer. The blue light above changed his face from blue to purple to white and back to blue again, and then his eyes looked up and met Ruth's.

But she did not focus on him. His face became a surprised blur in front of her as Michael whirled her around, and she did not even look back. She felt protected in the security of his powerful arms and did not care what Clyde thought, or even whether he cared at all.

And then, too quickly, the music was over and Michael was leading her back to Kitty.

"May I have this dance, madam?" he asked, bowing slightly.

"Oh, Michael, we're going to wear you out!" Kitty exclaimed, but she followed him out on the floor. Ruth had barely sat down when she heard a voice saying, "Ruth, would you like to dance?"

She turned and faced a somewhat short boy from

her science class, who looked decidedly better in a suit and tie than Ruth remembered him from school.

"Sure," she said, hoping she didn't sound too awfully grateful.

"Big crowd," Eddie Galvin said, slipping his arm around her. "I hear it's the most popular dance of the year next to the prom."

"The decorations are nice too," Ruth offered, as they began moving sedately about the floor.

"Who you with?"

"Michael Burke," Ruth told him, not knowing how else to answer.

"Never heard of him. Go to this school?"

"He's graduated," Ruth said proudly.

"Hey, you like your men old!" Eddie said, and laughed a little.

"He's a nice guy," Ruth said.

She caught Kitty's eye across the floor and winked, but did not look any longer for Clyde. She let herself be swept up by the music, guided by her partner, conscious only of the rhythm of the dance and the sparkle of the streamers as they twisted above her, catching the light.

Eddie led her back to her chair as Michael was returning with Kitty. Ruth introduced them.

"May I have another dance later, Ruth?" Eddie asked, before moving on.

"Sure," she told him.

Kitty and Ruth went down the hall to comb their hair and give Michael a rest. Kitty lifted her wrist and drank in the fragrance of the gardenia.

"I feel positively rich," she said.

"Having a good time, Kitty? Really?"

"This is the most wonderful thing that ever happened to me, Ruth. And people have been *looking* at me. Boys are noticing."

"It's only the beginning," Ruth assured her and was glad she'd said it. In fact, what a very nice thing to have said!

Holding a cluster of blue balloons, Ruth walked down the path from the school beside Michael and Kitty, glad she had come, delighted they had asked her, grateful that they had insisted. Small groups of couples scattered out in various directions, and the few who could afford to come in cars cruised slowly around the block, waving to friends and picking up passengers.

Kitty had wrapped herself in one enormously long silver streamer, circling her body at an angle from shoulders to knees. Michael said she looked like King Tut, come to put a curse on Clyde Heidelberger, and that started the giggles again. By the time they had reached the corner, the streamer had sunk down around Kitty's ankles, forcing her to take small mincing steps, and they all howled.

"Well," said Michael, when Kitty finally unwrapped herself, "where shall it be, ladies? Filet mignon on Rush Street? Or shall we just get in our limousine and cruise the North Shore till we see something that appeals?"

"Listen, Michael, you don't have to take us anywhere," Ruth said quickly, determined he should not spend anything more on them. But Kitty had a surprise she'd kept even from Michael.

"Daddy said the treat's on him," she announced. "He said I could bring you back to the store, and you could have anything you wanted to eat."

"No kidding!" Michael stopped and stared at her. "Kitty, you're a doll! You sure? I want a salami and cheese on Russian rye with a big blob of horseradish. How does that sound?"

"Terrible," said Kitty, "but there's no accounting for taste!"

They all laughed again.

"Brother!" said Michael, walking faster. "I don't know how long it's been since I had a sandwich like that."

The clouds swirled above them in the moonlight, and the wind—though cold—had a certain softness about it; spring was definitely in the air.

Michael shuffled to get in step with Kitty and Ruth and then, with their arms around each other, the three walked briskly down the street, swaying from side to side.

Lorenzo's market took on a different character at

night. Kitty left off the overhead light and turned on a lamp behind the counter instead. The glow cast tall shadows against the far walls where cans of cherry peppers, clam sauce, and chick peas crowded the shelves. Having been closed up for the evening, the store emitted a powerful fragrance of sardo cheese, pickles, spicy bologna, onions, hot sausages, and yellow apples—all mingled with a whiff of sweet almond pastry. Like silent customers, barrels of dry chestnuts, fava, and roasted ceci peas stood in a line beside the showcase, and boxes of stiff boneless salt cod crowded against the cans of olive oil on the floor. At eye level, Ruth focused on the dark-haired ladies that graced the packages of tortellini, and she thought how much more beautiful Kitty was than any of them.

Kitty slipped behind the curtain that divided the store from the apartment and returned with two kitchen chairs for Michael and Ruth. Then she climbed on the high stool behind the counter and spread out their napkins before them.

"Anything you like," she said.

Michael stood in awe for a moment of the temptations around him. "It's not really fair, Kitty. Your dad doesn't know how much I can eat."

Kitty merely laughed and popped a black olive in her mouth, glad to be able to contribute something to the evening.

Ruth had not realized until now how hungry she

had been. Was it months since she'd been able to eat until she was really full? It wasn't until she saw the jars of triangular crackers, the white cheese, the oranges and rolls and cookies and custards that she realized how impoverished the food on their own table must look to Michael.

"This," Michael was saying, setting a salami on the counter for Kitty to cut, "and this . . . this . . . a little of this . . . and some milk. That's the appetizer. It'll get me started."

Kitty began slicing the meat, and Michael leaned his arms on the counter.

"Kitty, how come you're not big and fat? If my Dad owned a store, I swear I'd eat all the time."

"I do!" Kitty said earnestly, "but it all goes into height! That's the story of my life."

Michael reached for the crumbs of cheese that had fallen on the counter. "My mother was even taller than you are and my Dad three inches taller than that. You know what he told her on their first date? He said, 'I've been waiting for a girl like you to come into my life from the day I was born, and now you're here.' And he proposed on the spot."

Ruth was glad that Michael told that story, whether it was true or not. In fact, she wondered if she shouldn't take her sandwich outside and leave the two of them alone. But they were soon laughing about other things, and the coziness of the little circle of chairs, the glow of the last remaining coals in the stove, the light of the lamp, and the delicious taste of mustard in her mouth kept her where she was.

She was conscious of eating faster than necessary, and she tried to slow down. When had she started eating like this, taking food in great gulps? She desperately wanted a second sandwich and was relieved when Michael asked for one first. Guiltily she thought of Dawn and her parents and the beans and potatoes diet. She knew how fond her father was of salami and how very long it had been since he'd had any.

Ruth and Michael said little while they ate, quick to catch the slightest crumb that rolled down on their napkins.

"You're still hungry!" Kitty guessed as Michael wiped his hands.

"Let's just say I'm resting," he answered, leaning back in his chair and propping his feet up on a potato sack. "Man, Kitty, I'm going to tell Mom all about this feast when I write her again. If I tell her everything I ate, she'll move the whole tribe to Chicago." He pulled out a comb from his pocket, folded a piece of paper over the edge, and began humming a tune on it. Then he put the comb down and sang the words:

Frankie and Johnnie were lovers!
Oh, Lordy, how they could love!

> They swore to be true to each other,
> Just as true as the stars above,
> He was her man,
> But he done her wrong.
>
> Frankie went down to the corner,
> Just for a bucket of beer,
> She said to the fat bartender,
> "Has my lovin'est man been here?"

This time Kitty and Ruth joined in:

> He was her man,
> But he done her wrong.

Ruth put her feet up beside Michael's as the song went on. Halfway through, a policeman walking by outside stopped and put his face to the window. Kitty waved, and he waved back, smiled, and went on; and the song continued without missing a beat:

> "I don't want to cause you no trouble,
> I don't want to tell you no lie;
> But I saw your man an hour ago
> With a gal named Alice Bly,
> And if he's your man,
> He's a doin' you wrong."

When Ruth thought the song was over, Michael added a verse she had not heard before:

> This story has no moral,
> This story has no end,

This story only goes to show
That there ain't no good in men,
They'll do you wrong,
Just as sure as you're born.

She thought of the man who had swindled Mr. Maloney, and the way her father had lost his job. She even thought of Clyde Heidelberger. But as long as there were fellows around like Michael, the song couldn't be true.

"Kitty," said Ruth, "and Michael . . . this has been just the nicest evening."

"Wait. It's not over yet." Kitty got up and went back to the cooler. This time she took out a whole cheesecake.

"Oh, Kitty, no! You don't dare cut it!" Ruth gasped.

"I asked Daddy especially about it, and he said we could each have one piece," Kitty insisted.

"Kitty, I'll bet your family doesn't get to eat cheesecake often."

This time Kitty didn't answer, but carefully cut three pieces.

Had she ever tasted it before, Ruth wondered as the sweet creamy flavor filled her mouth, settling down on her tongue while she rolled it around. Perhaps, a long time ago, before the Depression began. She couldn't remember. It was terribly expensive. She wanted it to last forever and ate very slowly.

"It's better with cherries on top, but we don't have any," Kitty apologized.

"Honestly, Kit," said Michael, "you mean the Lorenzos eat this way every night—imported salami, gourmet mustard, cheesecake. . . ."

Kitty smiled, a little embarrassed. "No, not really. I guess we all eat the same things, don't we? Spaghetti, beans, potatoes . . . tons and tons of potatoes. . . ." And Ruth understood. The food that night had been as much a treat for Kitty as it had been for them.

Michael felt another song coming on, and improvised:

> Kitty, you're the sweetest girl I know,
> Kitty, you're the sweetest girl I know.
> Yeah, you made me walk from Chicago, baby,
> Down to the Gulf of Mexico.

Kitty laughed. "That'll be the day."

"Don't worry," Ruth told her. "As long as you feed him cheesecake, he's not going anywhere."

Michael sat up and put his hands on Kitty's. "It was a great night, Kitty. I'm glad you asked me to go. Thank your Dad for a great dinner. It'll last me all through tomorrow."

"It *was* fun, wasn't it?" Kitty said and walked to the door with them. "Ruth, I hope old Heidelberger saw you dancing with Eddie Galvin and Michael and turned green with jealousy."

"Oh, who cares about Clyde?" Ruth said, not quite convincingly. But for this one night, at least, she *didn't* much care.

They walked home together, she and Michael —watching the clouds rushing over the moon, eager to have done with night and start a new day. And when they reached the corner, Ruth held up the blue balloons and let them go, one at a time, watching them rise toward the dark night sky.

"If I keep them, they'll just shrivel away," she said. "I'd rather remember them as they are now and always wonder what happened to them. Sometimes it's better not to know."

CHAPTER 8

June 8, 1933

Dear Diary:

Today was the first day of summer vacation. I spent the whole afternoon looking for a job, but everyone said no. Some stores even have signs in their windows so you won't bother to come in asking. Mother heard that Mrs. Cranston, over by the park, was looking for a cleaning girl so I went by to see her, and she hired me for Saturdays. She's got eleven rooms, though, and her kitchen's a mess. The thought of cleaning someone else's bathroom makes *me sick, but I guess I'm lucky to have a job at all. The only reason she hired me instead of an older woman was because she could get me cheaper. Kitty's still looking. It would be great if we could earn enough to see the World's Fair, but I doubt we'll be able to afford it.*

I thought when summer came, things would be better, but right now it seems worse than it's ever been. Dad only made three dollars last week, and a chicken costs twenty-five cents. A social worker's coming over tomorrow to see if we qualify.

The lady was short and rather young. She wore thick glasses, and if it weren't for those, Ruth thought, she might be pretty. Her hair was arranged in big puffs on either side, and she wore an engagement ring on her finger.

She sat down in the green chair, the one with the broken spring, and as the cushion creaked and sank low, she jotted it down in her notebook. All the while she talked, in fact, her eyes scanned the room, and her pencil was busy making notes.

"I thought you understood that both husband and wife were to be present for the interview, Mrs. Wheeler."

"I'm sorry," Mother said. "I just didn't know that. Joe's out trying to sell again this morning. Maybe I could fill out the forms for him."

Ruth sat motionless on the couch, listening uneasily. Dawn came edging down the hall stairs, despite Mrs. Wheeler's instructions to play in her room. Mother glanced at her fiercely, sending her scooting back up again.

"We'd have to have his signature," Miss Elderry said. "I'll go ahead and make the report, and if the assistance comes through, your husband will have to come down to the office and sign for it." She stopped and studied her notes. "Two daughters?"

"Yes."

"And there's a young man living here also?"

"Yes. My . . . nephew."

Ruth turned and looked at her mother, but Mrs. Wheeler avoided her eyes.

"He's a dependent, then? Your husband is his sole support?"

"Yes . . ." Mother hesitated. "Well, sometimes he gets work washing dishes or something."

Ruth sat staring down at her hands, turning them over in her lap as though she had never seen them before. Hard times made hard people, but she hadn't expected this of Mother.

"I'll have to ask to look around," Miss Elderry said, and seemed somewhat embarrassed herself. "I know it's personal, but I have to see your clothes closets."

"The clothes closets?"

"Yes. It's a nuisance, I know, but I have to make a report."

Mrs. Wheeler led the way upstairs. They entered Ruth's room first. Ruth stood outside, her cheek against the wall, hot with humiliation.

"There are a few very nice dresses in here," she heard Miss Elderry say.

"They came from her cousin," Mrs. Wheeler explained defensively. "They're the only nice things Ruth's had for several years. I can give you the name of my sister. You can write her yourself. We never had the money to buy Ruth new things for high school. And a girl her age . . . it's embarrassing when she has to go to class in old things of her mother's. . . ."

"Mrs. Wheeler, there are some girls who don't go to class at all because they have virtually nothing," Miss Elderry said.

Ruth went downstairs and sat by the bay window. She wasn't sure why she always came here when she felt torn up inside. Perhaps because Mrs. Hamilton's house, viewed through the window, seemed to sit there so solidly, unchanged, year after year, surrounded by tall locust trees that were unaffected by bank closings and stock markets and the price of chicken.

Mr. Maloney sat on its side steps as usual, like a monument himself—unmoving, unblinking, tipping at an uncomfortable angle. Mrs. Hamilton said he'd been drinking more and more, and she might have to put him out. Ruth felt only pity. Anybody living and breathing in 1933 had her profound sympathy, and what he clung to for comfort was his own business.

The footsteps overhead moved slowly from room to room. Then the conversation drifted down to the kitchen, and finally Miss Elderry was back in the hallway, preparing to leave.

"I'll send in the report, Mrs. Wheeler, but I just don't see how you can possibly qualify for relief. I had no idea you were buying your home, and we don't consider applicants until they have exhausted every possible source of savings. I'm afraid you misrepresented your family's situation in your letter."

To Ruth's horror, her mother began to sob. Her mouth opened wide without making a sound, showing dark places where her teeth were going bad. When she tried to speak, sobs came instead. Ruth had never remembered her mother crying before all the troubles began. Now she cried so easily. The Duchess—crying.

"Please," she said, when she could talk again. "I'm no beggar, but now I'm begging. We haven't had anything but beans and bread and potatoes for two weeks. The girls. . . ." Here she stopped and choked back more tears. "No girl should have to live this way, and it's no diet for a young man. We're hungry, Miss Elderry. We worry all the time. My husband's got back trouble and sometimes he can't go out selling at all. We didn't have enough coal all winter to barely get warm. The house is all we've got, and it's a struggle to keep up the payments."

Ruth could tell by the way Miss Elderry shuffled the papers in her hands that it was necessary to stay detached. She saw so many cases in a day. Each morning she probably went from house to house, hearing the same stories. And yet, she was human, too. She reached out and touched Ruth's mother on the arm.

"I understand, Mrs. Wheeler. Believe me, I know what you must be going through."

A lie, thought Ruth. *She couldn't possibly know. She and her silky dress and thin gray stockings and the shiny shoes. She doesn't know at all.*

". . . but there are others far worse off," Miss Elderry continued. "You have the house, for instance. If things got bad enough, you could sell it and live off the equity for awhile. That's more than many other families can do."

"But who would buy it?" Mother protested. "Everybody is selling. No one wants to buy. And where would we go?"

"Surely you have relations," Miss Elderry said. "What about the family who sent the nice dresses?" She dropped her pencil in her purse and put one hand on the doorknob, eager to leave. "These are hard times for a lot of people, Mrs. Wheeler, and I'm sure you understand that families who have nothing at all receive first priority. And there are so many of them. . . ."

When the social worker had gone, Mother passed through the living room where Ruth was sitting. Neither spoke. They knew what the Depression had done to them, and it only hurt to talk about it.

"Don't tell your father that she was here, Ruth," Mother said finally, and that was all.

It was time, Ruth decided, to do something she had only fantasied before. Sometimes when things were at their worst, she sat here at the window and saw the whole scene before her eyes, as though looking out upon a stage. Mentally, she had kept it in reserve as a last resort, when everyone else was powerless. Now, it seemed, even Michael had lost his optimism, because he'd lost his job as well. The brother of his boss was out of work, and so he was given Michael's job loading trucks. All Michael had left was his dishwashing job on Saturday nights. For the last month he had gone out every day, six days a week, looking for steady work. Everywhere he went, he said, the story was the same: no work, and if there was, a man with family responsibilities would get picked first.

And so some days he went down to the Loop and stood on a corner selling Two-in-One shoe polish to the luckier men in the Palm Beach suits and Panama hats, and once, when he got a temporary job distributing samples of breakfast cereal, the family ate Corn Flakes and Rice Krispies for a week.

The endless hours of waiting, however, were beginning to show on him—waiting in line, waiting for a number, waiting to be called, waiting for forms to be filled out—chronic, endless, futile waiting. He didn't take it out on the Wheelers, but shut himself away from them instead. Occasionally he would go straight to his room when he got home in the evenings and stay there, and Mrs. Wheeler learned to let him be. On these days she left his dinner warming in the oven, and he would come down later and eat alone.

It was time to do something new, something bold, like Roosevelt said, Ruth decided.

Mother had gone down to the basement to start another load of wash. Ruth went quickly up to her room and put on the blouse with the large patch under one sleeve, the skirt that had been widened by a piece down one side. She slipped on the stockings with a hole at the ankle and her oldest pair of shoes. Then she washed her hands meticulously, combed her hair, and, taking a dollar of the two she owned, went quietly outside and shut the door.

She had to ask the streetcar conductor the route, and repeated his instructions about transferring to be sure she had them right. If she made a mistake, it would cost an extra fare.

As the car whirred north toward the Loop, Ruth breathed deeply several times and tried to stop the shaking. She struggled to keep her mind blank, to forget about what she was doing until she got there, but her thoughts refused to let go. What would Mother say if she knew? What would *Father!* . . . For some reason the large painting of Joan of Arc in the school library came to mind—Joan in her suit of armor. How had she felt at that moment? How had she felt at the stake?

She recognized several of the department stores, the clock on Marshall Field's, and a restaurant where Father had taken her once, several years ago, when she met him downtown one Saturday. Only four more blocks, three, two, and suddenly it was time to get off. She was glad for the chance to move her legs and walk off the tension and started quickly down the sidewalk on the fringe of the crowd. An apple peddler held up a piece of fruit as she passed, and she averted her eyes. She wanted nothing to distract her now, no unnecessary conversation till she walked in that door.

The storefronts were very familiar now . . . the shoeshine parlor, hat shop, the cafeteria with the high-backed chairs, the bookstore, and suddenly . . . there she was. The sign had been changed and it didn't seem right. It wasn't fair.

She opened the door and made her way through a cluster of sofas and armchairs toward a salesman who was coming over.

"Yes, miss?"

"I'd like to see the manager . . . the owner," she said.

"Mr. Reed? He doesn't work out on the floor. Something I can help you with?"

"No. I'm afraid I have to see him."

"He's awfully busy, miss. We're not hiring, if that's what you're here for."

"It's a personal matter," Ruth told him. She'd been prepared for that.

"I'll see if he's in."

Ruth followed him back through the endless clutter of furniture. There were no straight aisles to the office in back, and they zigzagged this way and that, past beds and dressers and rocking chairs, until they came to a frosted glass wall. The salesman stuck his head around the partition.

"Myrtle, is Mr. Reed still here?"

Ruth waited, the throbbing growing louder in her ears.

"He was a moment ago. Has a conference at three."

"Well, there's a girl out here—says it's a personal matter."

There was silence from behind the glass wall. Ruth was sure they were communicating by signals. A head rose up over the glass and a young woman with a short blonde bob peered at Ruth, then ducked down again. More whispering.

"Come on back, honey," the woman called out. "Won't take more than a minute, will it? Mr. Reed's real busy today on the new inventory."

Ruth went on around the glass and followed the blonde woman to a door at the rear. The secretary knocked, then opened it a crack.

"Mr. Reed? A girl out here says she's got to see you." She turned to Ruth again. "What's your name, honey?"

"Ruth Wheeler." The words barely came out.

"Ruth Wheeler," the secretary said, sticking her head in the door again, as if somehow that made it confidential.

"Hell, Myrtle. I haven't had any lunch yet," came an exasperated male voice. "Every time I turn around. . . ."

"She won't take more than a minute," the woman said, withdrawing her head again and pulling Ruth toward the door.

"I can wait," Ruth said, fearful of facing a man with an empty stomach. But it was too late. She was in and the secretary closed the door behind her, leaving her alone in the room with Mr. Reed.

He was a big man—very tall, with large hands and broad shoulders. He looked too big for the store somehow. He should have been working for Smythes. He was standing by his desk, shuffling through some papers. Glancing up at Ruth for a minute, he nodded, and went on shuffling.

"Yes?"

Ruth knew at once that this was a mistake. She knew at once that this was not the right man, not

the right mood, not the right time, but she had to
see it through.

"I'm Ruth Wheeler, Mr. Reed," she said. "Joseph Wheeler's daughter."

"Don't think I know him. What's the problem?"

"Well, it's about my father. You bought the store
from Mr. Lawson, didn't you?"

The big man looked up. "Not me. I'm only the
manager here. If it's Mr. Martin you want, you'll
have to write Indianapolis."

Why did she keep on talking? It was so futile.
But there was nothing else to do.

"My father used to be the manager of this store
before it was sold. He was the manager for nineteen
years, and he knows all about furniture and customers and everything."

The man knew what was coming. He stood
watching her, fingertips resting on his desk.

"He still doesn't have a job, Mr. Reed, and I was
wondering if...."

Mr. Reed interrupted. "Little lady, I admire
your pluck, but I've got eleven salesmen to look out
for—men that have worked with me for a long
time. If I could hire everybody in Chicago who's
out of work, believe me, I'd do it tomorrow. But I
can't." He picked up two of the papers, placed them
in a folder, and started toward the door. Ruth didn't
move. She couldn't. Her feet felt like blocks of concrete.

Mr. Reed opened the door and hesitated. "You had lunch? You want a sandwich or something?"

Perhaps he thought she would faint. Perhaps it would help if she could.

"No, thank you." Ruth stood up. "We're terribly poor right now, Mr. Reed. If you could just hire him part time...."

He was cold now. "I've got three more men out there on the floor than I really need because I don't have the heart to let them go. I'm sorry, sweetheart, but I'm just keeping my head above water. That's about it."

He held the door open for her. Ruth walked out through the office. The secretary half turned and watched her go, and Ruth was sure that she was staring at the piece Mother had sewn in the side of her skirt. Out through the showroom where the salesmen were arguing about something, around the maze of furniture to the front door, and then out upon the sidewalk, among the well-dressed businessmen and ladies in white hats and silk dresses.

She wouldn't have minded if Father had been hired. She would have gone anywhere, dressed any way, if only it would have helped. But it hadn't. She had spent most of the little money she had left, as well as her last bit of hope, on a ridiculous streetcar ride.

This was a part of life she could not control. Persistance had not paid off. Cleanliness and politeness

had not helped. Dressing in rags had gotten her no-
where. And yet, like Annie Scoates, she knew that
she would keep going. Ruth realized that for the
first time in many years she could think of the
small, scrawny woman without disgust.

Ruth rubbed a wet cloth over the cake of Bon
Ami she held in her hand, making a white paste, and
then wiped the big window with it. Mrs. Cranston
was watching from the hall, and Ruth hated the way
the woman followed her about making little com-
ments and suggestions. If Mrs. Cranston had so
much time, why didn't she do her own work?
Then Ruth wondered why she even dared think
such a thing when the family needed every nickel
she could earn.

"The corners, dear, way up high. Don't forget
the corners," Mrs. Cranston said, her red curls bob-
bing as she spoke. There seemed to be no neck at all
on the woman—the heavy flesh of her jowls simply
joined up with her chest in a single crease. Ruth
tried to avoid looking at her. "If you need it, there's
a step stool in the garage. I do like my corners to be
clean."

"I think I can reach them if I get up on my toes,"
Ruth said, and stretched as high as she could till her
fingers reached the upper edge of the window
frame.

"Good. When you finish, dear, go over the bathtub again, will you? It's just not quite clean enough, I'm afraid. And then you may leave. I've a soup bone you can take to your mother."

The sound of the woman's heels on the heavy oak floor faded away as she went upstairs to inspect the bedrooms. Ruth sat down on the edge of a brown velvet chair to wait for the Bon Ami to dry, and the opulence of the furniture made her own living room seem even shabbier.

There was no change in sight. One day followed another with its lack of laughter and constant worry. She would grow up not having had much of a girlhood at all. If she became a teacher, where would she get her enthusiasm? If she married, it would probably not be till she was thirty-five and her own teeth were falling out. What boy could afford it sooner? Where were the chiffon dresses and the gay rides in a boyfriend's automobile, the canoe trips and picnics? She would go into her twenties having had none of it, and would have no photographs to show to her children or students, no souvenirs, no memories. She would be old far before her time.

Mrs. Cranston was coming back, and Ruth began rubbing the glass clean.

"Did you sweep the back porch, too, dear?"

"Yes, Mrs. Cranston."

"And the basement stairs?"

"Yes."

"All right. Here's your money and the soup bone. There's some good mutton left on it. I wrapped it up for you and put it in a bag . . ." She lowered her voice to a conspiratorial whisper. ". . . so the neighbors won't know. I'll see you next Saturday, and you might want to come a little early because I'm having a dinner party for sixteen, and there will be so much to do."

Ruth walked home slowly, tired, conscious of the grime on her arms, and wished she'd washed up before leaving. She had the feeling that Mrs. Cranston did not like her using the bathroom more than necessary and was never sure just which towel she should use.

What did people like the Cranstons serve at a dinner for sixteen, she wondered. Roast beef, perhaps, or a leg of lamb with mint jelly. Duck, possibly, or even pheasant. What was pheasant under glass? What were caviar and cherries jubilee? Strange how her mind seemed to focus on food. Each time she came, she could not resist peeking in Mrs. Cranston's electric Kelvinator to see all the food she kept in it—certainly enough to last the family a month.

When she reached home, she found her mother haggling with the junk man. Mrs. Wheeler was standing on the back porch, surrounded by boxes of rags, and Dawn was dragging even more up from the basement. It was all too depressing. Ruth went upstairs to wash.

As she came back down, she found Michael waiting for her on the landing.

"I've got to run over to the store," he said. "Come along and keep me company."

"I'm tired," Ruth protested.

"I'm irresistible," Michael teased. "Come on."

They set out at a brisk pace, enjoying the gentleness of the early summer sun, and Ruth decided she wasn't as tired as she'd thought.

"Your mother tell you that some guy came to see you this morning?" Michael asked.

Ruth didn't even turn her head. "If it was Clyde again, I don't even remember his name. He thinks we can start all over again, as if nothing had happened. I don't care what he says."

"Yeah, but I wouldn't hold it against him forever, Ruth. He feels like a first-class jerk and is trying hard to make up. Anyway, it wasn't him."

"It wasn't? Who, then?"

"Somebody named Eddie. Eddie Gallagher or Green or. . . ."

"Galvin? Eddie Galvin? The boy you met at the dance?"

"Yeah, that's who it was. I thought he looked familiar."

Ruth felt a little quiver of excitement, but she let it die, wary of making too much of it. "What did you tell him, that I was cleaning somebody's house?"

"Now, Ruth, I wouldn't do that. No, I just said you weren't in and we expected you back this evening. How's that?"

Ruth smiled. "You did okay. What'd he say?"

"That he'd come back again, maybe tomorrow."

They reached the grocery, and Ruth sat down on the bench outside while Michael went in to make his purchase. When he came out, a package under his arm, he tossed a Tastyeast candy bar in her lap.

"Oh, Michael, it's been a year since I had one of these!"

"Enjoy it," Michael said, as they started home. "The last of the big spenders."

Ruth insisted that Michael take half, and for a few minutes they said nothing, too busy enjoying the sweetness of the candy.

"You know what, Michael?" Ruth said at last. "Mrs. Cranston has so much food on the top shelf of her refrigerator that there's not even room for the water jar. I'll bet they have meat every night. Yet she's always talking about the awful price of butter and how expensive gasoline is and how she hopes she can make do with last summer's hat."

Michael grinned. "Yeah, you sure hear a lot of poor-mouthing these days. Used to be everybody tried to look richer than he was. Now the rich are all trying to look poor. Scared to death. Some of 'em even carry guns, I heard. Lot of the women who used to drive up to the door of Marshall Fields and have the doorman park their cars take the street-car now—don't want anybody to know they've got money."

"Michael, what do you think will happen to us? I mean, to you and me and Kitty and everybody? What if things really don't get better? If I had to live like this another five years, I don't think I could stand it."

She expected him to say something smart in return, but he turned serious instead.

"Don't ever say you can't stand it, Ruth. It's that kind of thinking that makes the big wheels jump out of windows. What they don't realize is that they *can* stand it, because it only puts them down on a level with all us other folks, and we're not jumping out of windows. And if you have to go down a lot further yet before you hit bottom, just remember there're a lot of other people down there who are making it somehow. That's one thing I learned from the jungles."

They reached home, and Michael casually slid the package on the kitchen table.

"What's that?" Mrs. Wheeler asked curiously.

"Dinner," Michael said, grinning. "It's on me tonight. I just wanted you to have it."

Ruth stared as her mother opened the white paper.

"Pork chops! Michael Burke, you know you can't afford pork chops!"

"Well, maybe not. But I bought them, so we

might as well cook them. Pork chops with boiled potatoes and onions. I've been thinking about it all day."

"Bless your heart, that's just what I'll fix!" cried Mrs. Wheeler. "Oh, won't Joe rave when he walks in the door and smells supper cooking! I've got some mustard greens, too. I'll put them right on, Michael, so you can enjoy your dinner before you go to work."

"Not this evening," said Michael. "I took the night off. I'll make up for it later."

Mrs. Wheeler stared at him. "Took the night off! Good heavens, Michael, you can't keep a job taking a night off when it's only one night a week that you work!" But it was no time for preaching, and soon the kitchen was alive with activity.

"Dawn, set the table, sweetheart. Here, Ruth, peel the potatoes and put some onions in with them like he said. Oh, Michael, you're just like our own boy. But you shouldn't have taken the night off. You know you shouldn't."

The pork chops were cooked carefully in the big iron skillet and delivered to the table with care. The family ate slowly, savoring the salty taste of the meat, holding the chops in their hands and gnawing off every bit of meat until the bones were dry. Dawn left the fat from her portion, and Mrs. Wheeler wrapped it and put it away to flavor the next day's beans.

Later that evening they listened to "Amos and

Andy" and worked a jigsaw puzzle of the Statue of Liberty that an uncle had sent them for Christmas. Joe Wheeler held Dawn on his lap and bounced her from knee to knee in his Sink the Ship game, sending her sprawling at last to the floor, laughing and shrieking, as the ship went down. It had been so long since Ruth had seen her father play that little game that she had actually forgotten it.

When Ruth got up on Sunday, she expected to find Michael reading the comics in the living room. By eleven o'clock, however, he still hadn't come down. She tapped on his door, but there was no answer. She went in. His bed was made, his closet empty, and there was a note and a dollar bill on the dresser.

Weakly, she sat down on the edge of the bed, her throat dry. He had left to join Roosevelt's new CCC program, the note said. He had already signed up and would be going to Utah to work in the forests. He would receive thirty dollars a month (here Michael had included an exclamation mark), and as soon as he got his first paycheck, he would send the Wheelers the other three dollars he owed them. He was leaving this way because he remembered how hard it had been to say good-bye to his family when he left Mendota, and he didn't feel that this would be any easier. But he thanked them for all they had done, the good times he had had, and hoped that Ruth and Eddie Galvin would "hit it off okay."

"P.S.," he wrote at the end: "Tell Kitty I'll miss her. If she isn't married by 30, I'll come back and ask her myself."

It seemed to Ruth that Michael had left when they needed him most. It especially hurt that he had left without saying good-bye, yet she understood. She knew that if he had told them he was leaving, they would all have tried to get him to stay. And it really was for the best; they could hardly afford to feed themselves now.

Like a succession of plagues, one disaster seemed to follow another. The washing machine gave out. Mrs. Wheeler returned to the old scrub board, and Ruth felt she could not stand to see her mother leaning over the washing machine that didn't work, rubbing not only the family's clothes on the board but her customers' clothes as well.

The following week, Mr. Maloney was found dead in the alley behind the house. He had gone out drinking, stumbled in the alley late at night, and died of overexposure, heart trouble, liver ailments, and more. Ruth was awakened about midnight by an ambulance siren and went outside to find her parents and Mrs. Hamilton on the back steps, watching the shadow of a body being lifted onto a stretcher. Mrs. Hamilton was crying.

"The Depression did it to him," she wept. "I've known Mr. Maloney for five years, and he was a fine, decent man when he took a room. Then, over

197

the years, it got so he didn't care for anything but drink. Caring never got him anywhere, though, and that's the truth."

Roosevelt and his ruby cuff links. What did he know about men like Mr. Maloney, dying in a drunken stupor in a back alley? People said that Roosevelt had made big changes, and that the country was moving again. Even Ruth's father said it. But Ruth saw nothing changing on her street, except that the holes were getting larger and the sidewalks continued to crumble. Chicago was spending millions on the World's Fair, but could not afford to fix its streets or pay its schoolteachers. As for Roosevelt, what had the bank holiday done for the Wheelers? Nothing. What were the Civilian Conservation Corps and the Tennessee Valley Authority and the National Recovery Administration but a bunch of initials?

Finally, what the family had feared most was upon them: they were four months behind in their mortgage payments and would lose the house unless they could pay at least $75 on it. In desperation they gathered every resource they had. Mrs. Wheeler sold a necklace inherited from her grandmother. Ruth sold her old bicycle. Father sold the large desk he kept in the bedroom. They gave up the *Sunday Tribune* and borrowed $25 from Mr. Wheeler's brother in Minnesota.

"Grace, we can't live this way," Joe Wheeler said. "This is it. I can't borrow again. We can't eat;

we can't pay the electric bill; we can hardly even stay alive unless I have a good week selling shoe-laces."

"What will we do, Joe?" Mother asked, and her voice sounded like that of a little girl.

"I don't know, Gracie. I just don't know."

Like characters in a play, they went about their daily tasks, waiting for the time when they couldn't pay anything at all and the house would be taken from them. Ruth wondered if she would look back on 1933 as the worst possible year in which to be alive.

She was coming out of Mrs. Cranston's one Saturday, her apron rolled up in a ball under one arm, when she came face to face with her teacher on the sidewalk below. She could not place her for a moment, could not understand what Miss Harley would be doing in this neighborhood.

"Ruth! How good to see you! I'm doing a survey for a toothpaste company to earn a little money over the summer. How are you?"

Ruth wiped her face with her arm, embarrassed to be caught looking so awful. "Okay, I guess. I've got a job, too." She nodded toward the Cranstons'. "I'm just getting off work."

"Well, let's sit a minute and talk," Miss Harley said, and they sat down on the low stone wall in the shade. "How are things going?"

"Bad," Ruth said, and instantly wondered if she

should have said "badly." But Miss Harley wasn't concerned with grammar.

"Things are pretty tough for your family?"

Ruth nodded, and then she found herself pouring out her soul. One thing about being bone-tired was that she just didn't care. She was too weary to worry about how it sounded.

"My father lost his job, and he's hardly had any work since. We keep selling things, but. . . ." Her voice quivered, but she didn't care. Let it shake. ". . . we keep getting further and further behind. I just know I'll never get to college. It's silly even to think about it. It will be just one more disappointment."

Miss Harley didn't even look at her. She sat staring out over the leaf-shaded street and thought about it. "Ruth, you don't know what the next few years will bring and neither do I. You think you can see what's ahead, but you can't. Things could get worse, it's true, but they could also get better. It's not silly to think about college and hope for it and work for it. That's the only way you'll ever make it if you do."

"I want to teach," Ruth said softly.

"I know you do."

"I've *always* wanted to teach, Miss Harley. It's all I've ever wanted."

"Then you must do it, Ruth."

"Sometimes . . . when I look at you in front of the

class . . . the way the students listen to you . . . the way they crowd around afterwards to talk . . . I think there couldn't be anything better in the world."

Miss Harley laughed a little and shook her head. "Oh, but that's the glory part, Ruth. We all like that. It's a very small part, however."

"What's the rest?"

"The rest is the real work. Most of the time the students aren't reaching out to me, the way it seems. I have to reach out to them—to go after them, to capture their imaginations by force. It's not enough, see, for them to accept me or listen to me or like me. I've got to accept *them*, and this means not only eager students like you, but the slow ones, the homely ones, the ones that mispronounce and fidget, the ones who never change their socks. They're all students of mine, and somehow I have to reach them all. That's the hard part. That's the challenge."

It was a side to teaching that Ruth had never thought about, and she wondered if she could do it.

"Do you think I'll make it, Miss Harley?" she asked timidly after they had sat quietly a few moments, enjoying the shade and the rest.

"I think you'll make it," her teacher said. "I don't know just how or when, but I really think you'll make something of your life. You wouldn't be happy unless you did."

"I've just got to," Ruth said, blinking back tears.

It was as though, at that very moment, she were making a vow in the presence of her teacher.

"But there's something else, Ruth, you may not have thought about. All these things that are happening to you—the troubles, the disappointments —are making you more of a person, whether you know it or not. The more you experience, the more you will be able to empathize with what your pupils experience. Everything that happens to you can be a lesson in life, and some of our best teachers have been through the most. There have been times in my own life when I felt I couldn't bear the way the cards were falling . . . it just wasn't fair . . . but I. . . ."

She stopped, her voice dwindling away. Ruth didn't dare breathe. Was it Broadway she was remembering? Was it the tubercular lover? Which of the rumors about her was it that made her blue eyes so distant now, that left her lips slightly parted, her face drawn? And then, just as suddenly, the eyes took on expression again.

". . . there has been nothing in my life, no matter how painful, that has not helped me become more humane. Do you know what I say to myself now when trouble comes? 'Welcome to the human race, Sue Harley,' I say. I'm not up on a cloud somewhere looking down, but right here with everybody else, a part of the grief and joy that the playwrights immortalized. And so are you. No matter what happens to you, Ruth, use it to grow on. There isn't a student—there isn't a person anywhere—that can't teach you something. If you open yourself to life, it will teach you more than you will ever learn in college. I promise you that."

Ruth didn't want Miss Harley to leave ever. Her head felt giddy, as though her mind had been stretched to the limit; and when her teacher stood up to go, Ruth wanted to reach out and hold her back. But she didn't. She just sat where she was, thinking. All these months she had felt it was so unfair—what was happening to her. All these months she had spent her energy fighting back, hating the way things were going, furious that they should be a part of her life. And she would still hate them, she knew, and still go on trying to make things better, but she would no longer look at them as wasting her time. Perhaps they had to be, and perhaps there would be more, and she would struggle with each one as it came along. But each would be a challenge, a lesson to be learned. Now, before she even got to college, she was studying to be a teacher by learning about life.

"Well, Ruth, I've got four whole blocks to cover yet this afternoon," Miss Harley said, smiling down at her.

"It's as though you were meant to come by today," Ruth said softly. "I never needed you more."

"Life is like that, too," her teacher said. "Besides

all the trouble and disappointment, things happen sometimes that couldn't be more perfect. I'm glad I saw you today too, Ruth. Sometimes, in my pupils—my very special pupils—I see myself as I used to be, and it's good sometimes to go back and visit."

Early in August, Ruth was sorting through her clothes to see which could possibly be worn again another year. She saw the dresses spread out on the bed before her, but all she could think about, it seemed, was food. A week ago she had taken a small piece of cake from Mrs. Cranston's refrigerator and had been tormented by guilt and embarrassment ever since. She suspected that Mrs. Cranston might have noticed somehow, though she had not said anything, and her silence and kindness embarrassed Ruth still further.

The doorbell rang, and Ruth's fantasies of food turned to Eddie Galvin. He had a habit of coming at odd times because he worked as a delivery boy for a liquor store and never knew when he would be in the neighborhood. Ruth felt easy with Eddie, almost as easy as she had with Michael. She was not instantly wild about him, the way she had been about Clyde, but she felt a quiet kind of liking for him that grew each time they were together.

She checked her hair quickly, straightened her blouse, and clattered downstairs to the door.

Annie Scoates stood there in a faded print dress.

In her arms she carried two huge sacks of fresh vegetables, and there was a box at her feet with still more. A man in a pickup truck waited at the curb, and Timothy sat shyly on the front steps, his face half turned away.

"Annie!" Ruth stared at the little woman, realizing that Annie had never been here before as company, only as help.

"Ruth, child, what a lady you are! I've brought you folks half my garden and hope you'll take it, after all you've done for Annie!"

"Well, I-I . . . please come in!" Ruth stammered, opening the door wide. She picked up the box and followed Annie out to the kitchen where they set the vegetables on the table. Out tumbled a profusion of turnips, carrots, potatoes, and squash. There were firm ripe tomatoes and a dozen onions. There were burgundy-colored beets, smooth green peppers, parsnips, sweet potatoes, and lima beans. Just looking at them made Ruth realize how terribly hungry she was, and she fancied the stew her mother would make.

"I had a good season, the Lord be praised," Annie said proudly. "A man down the road, he give me some seed, and the Lord must have breathed on it, 'cause it sure growed up good."

"Oh, Annie, Mother will be so happy."

"Where is she, child?"

"She's seeing about some alteration work to do

here at home. Dawn's out collecting bottles, and Dad's selling. They'll all be sorry they missed you."

"Well, you just tell 'em a neighbor offered to drive me over, so I can hardly stay more'n a minute. Got to thinkin' 'bout you folks and all you done for me, and thought maybe times wasn't so good for the Wheelers. Ruth, girl, let me look at you! You're thin, I declare! You're thin as sticks!"

Annie Scoates gripped Ruth by the arms and looked at her hard, and the familiar odor that seemed to haunt the woman surrounded her. Annie's hair, uncombed, was thinning, and lay plastered in little sweaty strands to her scalp. All her front teeth were missing but three, and there was a growth on one cheek that had gotten larger.

Ruth stared, as though she were seeing her own mother ten years hence, and for a brief moment she wanted to shove the woman away with her smells and her ugliness and the way she sucked back the saliva in her toothless mouth. But she didn't, for there was another part of her that wanted to touch Annie, to comfort her in return, to share with her feelings about what had been happening to them both.

Annie dropped her hands and looked around the kitchen. "My, how this place has changed since I cleaned house for your mother. Walls are cracked, paint chipping, linoleum worn through. Ruthie, it's *real* hard times, isn't it? You didn't tell old Annie, but somehow I just knew."

Ruth nodded, and suddenly, from somewhere inside herself, a feeling began that surged stronger and stronger till she could no longer contain it, and all at once she was crying, harder and harder, crying as her mother had cried the night she broke the thermometer.

Instantly two scrawny arms reached out and hugged her to Annie's warm chest, and Ruth threw her own arms around the woman's neck. She found herself being rocked back and forth, just as Annie had rocked her the day Charles died. Tenderly, Annie stroked her, cuddled her, and Ruth didn't care. *She didn't care.*

"Cry, Ruthie, go on, honey, and cry it all out. Annie knows," the woman crooned. "It's hardest on you folks that ain't used to it. Of all the women deserves a break, it's your mother. She stuck by Annie all these years when times were hard, and Annie's not going to forget that."

She rocked Ruth some more, making little comforting sounds in her throat, and Ruth found strength and reassurance in someone who really knew what it was like. She needed to cry, thirsted for it, finding almost a pleasure in the sound of her sobs and the knowledge that she could do it, that she could accept Annie's love and give her own in return.

"You all come out to see me again in September, and I'll have some sweet corn for you. Tell your mother to put away as much as she can for winter, it'll take some of the worry off her. There, Ruthie girl, you just cry it all out."

Ruth stood at the door a long time after the pickup truck had left, staring out into the empty street. The wall that had been there before, between Ruth and the old woman, was gone.

She would be a teacher, she was sure of it—sometime, somehow—a teacher of all the students, the eager ones, the slow ones, the homely ones, the ones that mispronounced and never changed their socks. She would learn to care as much for the dull ones as the bright ones, the Scoates's children or the Cranstons'. She would take dirty little boys with runny noses; ugly, cross-eyed girls with bowed legs; nervous, self-conscious boys who stole milk off of porches, and see beyond the self each presented in the classroom to what he might possibly become. And she would work to capture their imaginations by force, to help them become what they ought to be.

Welcome to the human race, Ruth Wheeler, she said to herself. The wall was gone, and she was so glad.

Epilogue

November 13, 1933

Dear Diary:

I know I haven't written for a long time, but wonderful things are happening. Last Monday, Daddy went down to register for Roosevelt's new program, the CWA—Civilian Works Administration, I think. There were so many men that it took eleven hours to sign them all up. But he made it! Daddy's in, and he gets a steady salary starting this week! Roosevelt said he wanted the first checks out in time for Thanksgiving. I'm so happy I don't know what to say. Dad goes around smiling and even laughs sometimes. Last night he brought home a pint of ice cream! He paid fifteen cents just for ice cream! We ate it right away, before supper. We didn't even care. Daddy said it was time to celebrate.

I honestly think the worst is over. I'm almost afraid to say it, for fear it might not be true, but so many more men are back on jobs—older men, too, like Father.

Mother says that what she wants most is to buy a doll for Dawn this Christmas. What I want most is for Mother to get her teeth fixed. Eddie's coming for dinner next week, and she always tries not to smile too wide when company's here for fear the spaces will show.

Maybe Roosevelt does understand about people like Mr. Maloney. It is possible, I know, to sympathize with somebody about something that's never happened to you—I mean to really imagine what it must be like. One thing is certain: the year is ending a lot better than it began. Dad says some day we won't even think about the Depression any more, we'll be worrying about somebody named Hitler.

I may work part-time next year if I need to. Miss Harley says that if I get permission from the principal, I can go to school two days a week and work three, clerking in the stores like some of the other *girls do. I hope I don't have to. I'd hate to miss any of her classes, but at least it's something to fall back on if we get desperate. Kitty's got to work, though. Her father gave credit to too many customers and almost lost the store, but I think they'll make it now. She got a letter from Michael last Friday. He says he's gained ten pounds and is strong as an ox. She still hasn't had a date with anyone else, but she said that just knowing that Michael thought she was pretty makes her feel a lot better about herself.*

I feel better about myself, too. Partly it's because Miss Harley talked to me about scholarships, and that might be one way I could get to college. But more than that, I'm changing inside. I know it. I can't believe I'm sixteen now—that's always seemed so grown-up and far away. I took a long look in the mirror this morning to see if the Depression had made me old. Annie said I was thin as sticks, but I've fattened up some since then. I don't think I look so bad—just a little wiser or something—a little more thoughtful, maybe . . . sort of around the eyes. . .

Historical note

The CWA program proved to be very costly, and there was widespread criticism. Finally, in mid-January, 1934, Roosevelt ordered it ended, and a million men were dropped from the payrolls every two weeks. Again they found work wherever they could until the Public Works Administration (PWA) was put into effect and many of the men were rehired. Slowly the economy began to recover.

On Friday, September 1, 1939, Adolph Hitler invaded Poland.